CROSSED BY DEATH

STITCHES IN CRIME
BOOK 1

ACF BOOKENS

1

I cinched the scarf more tightly around my head and
wedged the hard hat into place. I'd learned the hard way
that not covering my hair and my head could mean a
mess, sometimes a bloody one.

The doorframe appeared to be solid, and when I pushed
hard against the floorboards with my right foot, they held solid,
too. I walked into the Scruggs Store and crouched beneath the
collapsing roof. Not much left here I could safely search
through, but I was going to do my best. I'd paid good money for
this salvage job, and I was going to get what I could.

I'd driven past this old gas station all my life and had
mourned as the vegetation took it over and began to pull it
down over the past few years. I knew, though, that no one in
our rural mountain county was going to buy the place, not after
someone had been murdered there twenty years ago. A single
gas pump on a country road wasn't enough incentive to take on
that bad mojo.

It was a loss, though, because the station had been there for
almost a hundred years – first as a country store and then as a
welcome fueling spot twenty-five miles from the nearest city. I

was determined to not let it all disappear when the bulldozers parked outside knocked it down. My fifty dollars had gained me entry and rights to anything I could carry out before the station was destroyed, and I was going to get my money's worth while saving a bit of history along the way.

I was new at the salvage business, but I knew enough about local history and had watched enough *Barnyard Builders*, *American Pickers*, and *Salvage Dawgs* to feel like I could find the good stuff. I headed to the left toward what used to be the check-out counter and hit paydirt right away. The original counter was still there, complete with a hand-written sign about check cashing as well as a Virginia lottery sticker from somewhere in the last decade of the previous century. A few coats of poly on this baby, and it would make a great piece of wall art for someone who loved that 1990s feel or just wanted to relive their heyday.

A few good pries with my crowbar and I had the whole countertop sitting by the door ready to go. That piece alone was worth my investment, but I wanted to go a bit further in, see if maybe there was some old stock of soda or something. People paid ridiculous prices for skunked beer and flat Pepsi. The coolers were underneath some rafters, so I moved gingerly toward them. Most of the shelves were empty, probably raided before the building started to cave in, but I could see the glint of light off glass in the back. Jackpot! The overstock was still there, it seemed.

I picked and tested my way to a door that seemed to open behind the wall of refrigerated units and prayed it wasn't locked. I didn't feel like kicking in a door and bringing down the roof. Luckily, the knob turned, and I was in. Not cases and cases of old stock, but enough to turn a good profit. As I carried out a few boxes of soda and Yuengling, I thought about how tight the margin for a store like this must have been. The owner had to keep enough supply to satisfy customers' last-minute shopping needs – gallons of milk, snacks, a few packs of diapers probably – but not so much that he couldn't make a profit on what he stocked. It was hard going.

Maybe it was easier, though, since he and his family lived at the back of the store, like a lot of shop owners back in the day. I thought about what it would have been like to grow up in that little house, to have people coming by all times of day and night to get cigarettes or pick up a sandwich from the little kitchen in the back of the store. I might have loved it, and I knew my son, Sawyer, would have thrived with all those people to talk to. His extroverted tendencies were in diametric opposition to my introverted ones. But I thought it probably also would have grown tiring and tedious.

As I set a sixth case of Cheerwine by the door, I made my plan for a last foray into the store and then, hopefully, into the house behind. I could just make out a doorframe in the far back corner, and since I'd noted the exterior bathroom doors before I came in, I figured this must be the way into the house. The only problem was that I was going to have to crawl my way back there. My forty-six-year-old body wasn't much for crawling despite the fact that Sawyer was in a "Be a rhino with me, Mommy" stage.

Still, that little boy needed his mommy to buy him cheese crackers and milk, so crawl I did. And when it was necessary for me to be thinner than my crawling hips would allow, I shimmied my way like a snake and decided I wasn't going to suggest Saw and I try that animal imitation out.

I made it to the door, though, and I was hoping that the quick look I'd had at the house hadn't been deceptive. Luckily for me, this roof was still standing at its full eight feet. I levered myself to standing and looked around at what reminded me of the living room of my high school years. A big black television from before the age of flat screens sat in one corner, and in front of it, a couch with overstuffed arms and red plaid fabric was under a rumpled blanket and a throw pillow. It looked like someone had just gotten up from a Sunday afternoon nap.

A quick scan told me there wasn't anything worth hauling out of here, but I was glad to find that the exterior door was easy to open in case I did find anything. If only I had seen it before I covered my entire front in dust from my army crawl back there.

I made my way into the kitchen and felt sorrow hitch in my chest. A wire rack with moldy cookies was waiting next to a plastic tub designed just for cookie storage. My mom had the same one, and I loved coming home from school and raiding the freshly baked stash. Beside it, the mixer was bowl-less, and I saw the stainless-steel bowl in the sink, ready to be washed. A mug of half-drunk tea sat at the edge of the counter. Someone, probably a woman, probably a mother, had been interrupted in her work.

I took a deep breath and said a word of gratitude to that woman before I started flinging open cabinets. I only had a few more minutes before Saw or our Maine Coon cat, Beauregard, got bored of watching funny cat videos in the car or someone saw them and came to investigate who had abandoned their toddler and a giant feline in their Subaru Outback at a derelict gas station. It wasn't my favorite choice of things to do, but Sawyer was safely in his car seat, the car was locked, and Beau was better than any guard dog, especially since he weighed in at a solid twenty pounds under his copious striped fur. The plight of a working single mom required creative problem solving, and sometimes creative problem solving involved a guard cat.

I found some vintage cookie cutters and a set of Corel dishes that I quickly loaded into the dishpan I had emptied into the sink. If I couldn't sell them, then someone would appreciate the set at Goodwill. A few pottery mugs and really nice knife block I could use at home rounded out my haul from this room.

After I deposited those items on the small porch outside the living room door, I plunged into the first of the bedrooms. I didn't think there'd be much to salvage here since the clothing wasn't going to be old enough to be truly vintage, but I hoped to maybe find some children's clothes in good shape for Sawyer and maybe a coat for me. I hit the jackpot straight off. Lots of four T pants and shirts that would fit Saw in a matter of weeks at the rate his two-year-old body was growing and even a couple of pairs of shoes. I tried not to think of the murder when I was in this room, but I prayed for this little boy. Prayed he was okay in all the ways.

There looked to be only two more doors in the small hallway, and the one at the end of the hall was likely the bathroom. I hadn't been in many abandoned houses, but I'd learned the hard way that opening the bathroom door was a bad idea. I skipped that one and went on to the other bedroom.

The curtains were pulled tight, and while the light would have been helpful, I was in a hurry. I just headed for the closet with my flashlight and rifled through the clothes before pulling boxes down in case there were antiques or any particularly great caches of photos or mementos I needed to rescue. When I had started this work, I'd made a vow that I would try to return anything personal to the owners if I could, so I always salvaged photo albums, boxes of children's art, and any other pieces of family history I could. Then, I spent ten percent of the money I earned from selling the other things to try to get those back to their owners. I couldn't afford to do more than that in terms of shipping or ads in local papers, but I figured the least I could do was try that. Sometimes, it worked. Often it didn't, and if it didn't, I tried to console myself with the fact that maybe people just wanted to leave the past behind altogether. I probably would.

I didn't find a coat for me in the closet, but I did see a small jewelry box shoved up on a high shelf. I chuckled. My jewelry box was in exactly the same place because Sawyer had developed a deep interest in wearing – and breaking – every necklace I owned. I wasn't about to let him swallow my grandmother's diamond ring, not when that was our financial back-up as well as a precious memento of my granny.

I tucked the jewelry box under my arm and turned to swing my flashlight around the room. As my light swept over the bed, I saw a lump in the corner under the window. I thought it might be a pile of discarded clothes, and with winter coming soon, I found myself praying that someone might have discarded their coat over a chair. The fact that my heart was racing made me pray even harder.

I made my way around the bed to get a closer look, and I clenched my teeth to keep from screaming. A woman was sitting in an armchair, and she wasn't moving – not even breathing.

I stepped back, took a deep breath to push down the panic because I didn't want to alarm Sawyer, and walked out of the side door of the house.

It felt awful to have to drive away from that house, but there was no cell service for a couple of miles. I threw the jewelry box on to the floor below where Beauregard reclined like the prince he was and headed north toward town. As soon as my phone showed three reliable bars, I pulled into the nearest driveway and dialed 911.

"Yes, this is Paisley Sutton. I just found a dead body in the old store on Scotch Road."

The dispatcher, used to traffic accidents and reports of four-wheelers on the roads I imagined, was a bit flustered, but he managed to tell me he was sending officers and that I should wait there. I explained I was two miles up the road and would get back to the store as soon as I could. He didn't even ask why I'd left the scene. We all knew the mountains wreaked havoc with cell service.

"What we doing, Mommy?" Sawyer asked from the back seat.

"Mommy has to talk to the police, Love Bug," I said as I ripped open a packet of fruit snacks with my teeth and handed it to him as I simultaneously swung the car back onto the road toward the store. "You're going to get to see police cars!" My son loved anything vehicular, and I was counting on flashing lights and maybe a kind officer who would show off a siren to help my toddler through this change of plans. He was going to miss his playground time, and if these police cars didn't make up for slides, it was going to be a hard fight for a nap.

My maternal worries were mostly allayed though as Saw started bouncing in his seat as soon as he saw the blue flashing lights by the store, and when I pulled over and told him to wait patiently, he said, "I will, Mama," and craned his little neck to see the police officers in uniform.

I walked to the first officer I saw and introduced myself. "I found the body," I said, and the young black woman nodded. Then, she looked over my shoulder at the car. "Your son?"

I smiled. "Yeah, I'm a single mom, so he goes with me everywhere. He doesn't know what's happening, but he sure is excited about seeing police cars."

She snapped her notebook shut with such briskness that I had a flash of fear that she was going to scold me for neglect. Instead, she tilted her head at the car and said, "Mind if I sit with him?" She pointed to the radio and flashlight on her belt. "My guy loves my toys."

I felt a flood of relief as she headed toward the backseat of my car and knocked on the door before asking Sawyer if she could sit down. When she patted her knees and let Beau settle

in her lap while Sawyer squawked her radio to high heaven, I
knew he'd be fine and went to see what I could find out about
the woman inside.

An officer was on the front stoop of the store, and so I
walked up and tapped him on the shoulder. When he turned, I
recognized his face from the election posters I'd seen around
the county for the past couple of months. He was our new sheriff, Santiago Shifflett, the first Latino sheriff in the area, and,
thankfully, the man I'd voted for.

"Sheriff, I found the body." That was a sentence I hadn't
thought I'd utter even once in my life, but here I was saying it
again. "Want me to take you in?"

"Ms. Sutton, thank you for calling it in. We actually found
her already, but I would like to ask you a few questions." His
voice was kind but serious.

"Of course." I had prepared as best I could to tell my story
in the few quiet minutes of the drive back to the store. "Do you
mind if we sit though? Sawyer, my son, got up at five-thirty, and
the adrenaline is starting to wear off."

"Sure," he said. "That work?" He nodded toward the bull-
dozer at the edge of the lot and headed that way.

I climbed up in the seat, and the sheriff stood below. A
deputy brought over two bottles of water, and I gulped mine
down with gratitude. "What do you need to know?"

Sheriff Shifflett leaned against the tracks of the dozer, and I
felt a little of my tension ease. If he wasn't worried about getting
his uniform dirty, I felt like I could trust him. After all, I walked
around with some stain – food, poop, playdough – on my
clothes every day of my life. "Let's start with why you were in
the house."

I pulled out my business card with "Save The Story," the
name of my business, printed across the top. "I do historical
salvage from old buildings. The owners gave me permission to
go inside and take whatever I could." I gestured to the stack of

soda and beer beside the small circle of officers on the store's porch.

The sheriff glanced over his shoulder and then back at me. "You found soda?" There was a lightness to his tone, and I could just see the start of a smile in the corner of his mouth.

I smiled. "I know, right? People pay a lot of money for old soda."

"They want the soda itself? Not just the bottles?"

"It's kind of like having old toys in the original box. Original condition means more value, I guess." I shrugged. "I don't question it. I just buy groceries with it."

Shifflett pursed his lips. "Whatever it takes to pay the bills." Sometimes people said that with mockery, but the sheriff seemed sincere.

"Exactly." I then told him about searching the house and about going into the back bedroom. "That's when I saw her. I didn't touch anything, and I'm sorry I had to leave the scene but—"

"Cell service, I know." He turned and looked at the house. "Did you notice anything unusual in there?"

I looked back up at the store and then beyond it to the attached house. "No. I mean, it was disconcerting to go into that house and see that it was like the people who lived there had been abducted by aliens. But I assume they left a long time ago, like after the first murder."

The sheriff turned back to me. "You knew about that then? And you still went in?"

"Like I said, groceries." I'd grown up nearby, and the murder had been a big deal, especially because they thought it had been someone who frequented the store. "Besides, there's a story there, one that needs to be remembered, and not just the story of the murder, the first one, I mean. Those people had lives before and after the father of that family was killed. I wanted to remember that, to help other people remember that." I took a deep breath, surprised that I'd shared that much with this man I'd just met. It wasn't really relevant to the investigation, after all.

But the sheriff didn't seem put off at all when he turned back to me. "I get it. Part of why I do my job, too. Crime happens to people and is committed by people. It's not just a thing that happens or that happens in one moment and then is gone. It's the people involved that get my attention."

I studied the sheriff's face for a second and then nodded. But then, I heard Saw's call, "Mama!" and knew my time was limited. "I hate to ask, but can I take the things I gathered from the house?"

He shook his head, "I'm afraid not. They're part of the crime scene. But if you have a minute," he glanced over his head toward the car, "maybe you could show me what you were taking. It'll help us sort out the scene but also, hopefully, I can get it to you later."

I nodded. "Of course." I took a quick look at my car and saw the deputy handing Sawyer her radio and gauged I had about five more minutes. I quickly walked him through the store and pointed out the countertop and the cases on the porch before showing him my haul outside the door of the house. He made notes and studied each pile of goods.

But then, I heard Sawyer's wail and knew I needed to go. "Thanks, Sheriff. You have my number, so call if I can help further." I waved as I jogged around the front of the store.

I hurried back to the car, where Sawyer was working up a good tantrum. I thanked the officer, gave my son a kiss on the forehead, and then climbed into the car. Eleven fifteen – it was time for a picnic lunch before my toddler went into total meltdown.

2

On days when Sawyer and I had to be out of the house early, I planned for a picnic and then a car nap. Today I was especially glad for the string cheese, tangerine, and slices of ham in his backpack because there was no way we were settling in for a nap at home after all that excitement.

I drove up the road as Saw tried to bite Beau's tail. I gave thanks for a patient cat who would walk away rather than attack.

Luckily, it was just cool enough for the farmers' market pavilion up in town to be empty, and the sole picnic table that had not succumbed to too much weather was free.

Saw was bouncing as I poured Beau a bowl of water and then unstrapped my two-year-old from his seat. "Time for picnic," he said again and again as we made our way to the table. I did a quick sweep of the area for potential hazards: pile of gravel, drop off on the other side of pavilion, water drainage behind three layers of construction fence. If I wasn't careful, Sawyer would explore all of those in the time it took for me to scarf down my own ham and cheese sandwich.

Fortunately for all of us, including the maintenance crew I might have to summon from the county office building if my son crawled into that water pit, there was a large puddle nearby, and Sawyer busied himself by throwing rocks with one hand and eating cheese with the other. That small distraction gave me enough time to think back about the morning's events.

When the murder twenty years earlier had hit the news, it had rocked our rural county. We had violent deaths, of course, but they always seemed tied to specific things like drugs or domestic abuse. Those things were horrible, of course, but this murder had seemed random, out of the blue. No robbery even. For weeks, people couldn't talk about anything else.

Now, it seemed far too much of a coincidence that a second person would be found dead randomly in that same building. It only seemed reasonable that there was a connection between the two deaths.

That hypothesis led me down a stranger thought-trail as Sawyer headed toward the rock pile. Maybe someone was hoping to hide a body there because they assumed no one would be in the building before it was taken down. If that was the case, the person must have been aware that the building was about to be demolished, and I didn't think that information was widely known, but of course, in places with few people, gossip travels remarkably fast. But that didn't mean the death was connected to the building.

Maybe, though, someone wasn't hoping to hide the body. Maybe the two deaths were linked by more than just place. Maybe someone wanted to send a message or had some symbolic reason for leaving the body there. My train of thought went very dark at that point as I pondered serial killers and cults and all kinds of ugliness. I blamed the fact that I'd binged *Mindhunter* the past two weekends that Sawyer was with his dad. That show was great but all kinds of creepy too.

Sparing me from my own macabre reflection, Sawyer made

a beeline for the water hole, and I leapt into all the action my middle-aged body would allow and lifted a flailing forty-pound boy back over the orange fence he had just scaled like an American Ninja Warrior. It was time for a nap. I wondered, for a split second, how long it would be before self-driving cars were safe because that would be a true gift to the parents of small children who only napped in a moving vehicle.

PRAISE BE to the God of parents because Saw dropped off before we were even out of town, and I had a blissful two hours to wander the mountain roads, study the way yellow trees held their leaves against the black trunks and branches of their brethren, and ponder the Scruggs store.

I didn't know much about the murder that had happened there two decades previous, just that it had been the father of the family, Luther, and that the case had never been solved, at least not that I knew of.

As we rode along the Blue Ridge, I stroked Beau's head and made mental notes about what I needed to look up. I decided I would feature the building and its history in my next newsletter. Those newsletters were one of the things I looked forward to most about my work, and as my subscriber list had grown, I'd started getting to know the people who replied. Some of my readers were genealogists with a penchant for place, and some were historians who loved the facts of a building. But most of them were just ordinary folks like me who appreciated old buildings and the stories that lived in them. They would love to know more about the Scruggs Store, and I was happy to oblige.

When Saw's father and I had split up a year ago, I had needed to find a way to work and have my son along. The research-intensive historical articles I'd been writing as a freelancer were just not feasible since they required many hours a day to dig through archives and read books, so I'd taken to a more hands-on field – salvage. In some buildings, Saw could come along and actually help me – the boy was a natural with a hammer—and when the job was dangerous, my best friend, Mika, kept Saw at her shop in downtown Octonia. He loved playing in the bins of soft yarn.

Between online sales, pop-up shops in Charlottesville, and word-of-mouth, I was building a steady income, enough that Sawyer and I had just bought a house of our own. Apartment living – as convenient as it was – just wasn't ideal. We needed history around us and nature at our door. Beau needed that too because the mouse population in our apartment complex was just not up to par.

But as much as I longed to sit on our farmhouse porch for a couple of hours, instead of turning toward home when I saw Saw was starting to stir, I headed toward town and hoped that it wasn't one of Mika's yarn group days. A toddler and women trying to knit were not a good combination, at least not as far as the knitting was concerned.

Just as we parked on the street outside her store, Sawyer opened his eyes and said, "Apple juice please," and I handed back the tumbler I had filled from a juice box while on a particularly quiet road. I had learned through a succession of sticky trials that a squeezable box and a toddler are not a good combination.

I let my slow-waking son sit and drink for a few minutes while I wrote down the notes that I had accumulated in my mind. Everyone kept recommending those note-taking apps for my phone, but they weren't exactly ideal when a toddler was sleeping nearby.

Notes recorded, I peeked in Mika's windows and saw her and one other older woman sitting in the wingback chairs by the windows, yarn in hand. *Perfect*, I thought, and got Saw out of his car seat. Beauregard, recognizing his surroundings, hopped out and followed me to the shop door and then slid past me as I pushed it open with an elbow. He had a special bed in the back of the store, and he loved how people admired his sheer size and lustrous fur. If he could, I swore he'd be creating a line of Maine Coon-inspired yarn as a tribute to himself.

Saw wriggled out of my arms with less grace than Beau, but with equal enthusiasm, and barreled into Mika's lap, barely missing a lung puncture from a knitting needle. "Auntie Mickey," he squealed.

"Saw-Saw, I didn't know you were coming." Mika held him out at arm's length before pulling him close again. "It's so good to see you. Can you stay and help me unroll some yarn?" Mika and Saw had an understanding – he could unskein any yarn she gave him, but he couldn't do more than touch any other stock in the store. Regularly, she had him string out the yarn she was going to use for herself or for a knitting circle, and then, I'd sit around and talk with her as I rolled the loose yarn into balls that she then secured with painter's tape. It was a winning arrangement for us all.

Today, though, I was hoping Mika was okay with me skedaddling to the county courthouse. I was eager to dig into the deeds on the Scruggs store, and the presence of a toddler might just send our county clerk into cardiac arrest. She was a tad fastidious about records, a trait I appreciated unless it meant I couldn't get my hands on something I wanted. "Have time and space to keep your assistant for a couple of hours?"

Mika smiled at me as she stood and gave me a tight hug. "Sure. Everything okay?"

I nodded. It wasn't the time to talk about the murder, not with Sawyer near and the knitter still in the wingback. "I'll catch you up via text. Just need to go to the courthouse for a bit of research."

"We're totally good here." Saw was testing the drumstick

quality of the various knitting needles in a barrel Mika kept by the register. "I'll text you if we need a Mommy-vention."

"Thanks, Miks." I turned to the woman in the chair. "Wow, that's a gorgeous shawl. Sorry if my little tornado's presence disrupts your calm."

"Are you kidding?" she said. "I have nine grandchildren. I concentrate better when someone wants to show me something every fourteen seconds."

I laughed. This woman clearly knew toddlers. With a kiss on Saw's head and an abrupt "Bye" from him, I headed the two blocks to the courthouse. The day had stayed perfectly clear, and I studied the way a few leaves hung to the sheltered side of the maples along the way.

The county records room was one of my favorite places – big tables, heavy books, and pages and pages of history all waiting to be studied. I'd been there enough times to know just what I hoped to find, but I also knew that just because I hoped the records were there didn't mean they would be.

First, I had to find the plat number for the store then research the deeds to make a list of who had owned the property when. Then, scan any wills for those people to see what I could learn about the place. That information should be able to get me pretty far toward a clear timeline of the store, and then, with the names I gathered, I could send a few emails to ask about the people who had lived there. Soon, I'd have more than enough for a good newsletter article with links to more information.

The clerk's office was filled with the gentle thrum of office work that was typical for the space. People came here for only a few main reasons – marriage licenses, land title research for real estate activities, and historical and genealogical research. All of those were quiet activities, except for maybe the marriage license requests, which sometimes including a fair amount of giggling and, on rare occasions, loud kissing. Otherwise, the research room was a lot like a library, and after a morning tending a boundary-testing toddler, I was ready to sink into something that didn't need to be fed or washed and that could occupy my attention for more than three minutes at a time. I loved my son, but I craved space to go deep and let my brain sink into something for a long period of time.

I found the plat information on the store in no time, and within an hour, I had a full run-down on who had owned the store when, including in the 1990s when the first murder on the site had occurred. I also saw the deed of the current owners, George and Berlinda Jefferson and that they lived over in Richmond. I had known the Jeffersons owned the store because they had given me permission to salvage there once a high school friend had told me in passing at the grocery store that his crew had been hired to take it down. We had become friendly, if not yet friends, and I really liked them.

I expected the sheriff had already reached out to them about the morning's events, so I knew I wouldn't be bringing them news when I called. Still, I figured kindness dictated I wait and see what the investigation turned up before I contacted them to talk about the store's recent history. Besides, I wanted to read up on the first murder and be sure I understood the ins and outs of it before I went asking questions. In a rural community, it was best to be wise and informed before you started talking about a place's or a family's secrets.

So, I turned my attention to the early history of the store. The first time a building is shown on the plat for the land was in 1903, so I assumed – given the architecture of the building – that this was probably the year the store was built. I took the name of the owner at the time, the Elijah Scruggs for whom the store was still known, and went looking for wills.

It took a few minutes, but I eventually found reference to the store being willed to an Alice Scruggs in 1922. Alice was Elijah's daughter, and on the inventory for the will's distribution, the store and its contents are valued at two-hundred-thirty-eight dollars, which was a lot of money for a woman to inherit at the time, particularly a black woman. I felt a frisson of excitement for Alice and decided I would focus my story on her. I loved all history, but I particularly liked history that wasn't mainstream . . . which usually meant the history of women and people of color.

Then, with about forty-five minutes to go before I was due back to Mika's store, I took a quick scan of the other Scruggs wills, making notes of names and dates before carefully putting the books back on the shelves. Lifting these tomes always felt like a little bit of a workout, and my shoulders had a healthy ache as I waved a thanks to the staff and walked back out into the late afternoon.

As I strolled, my phone rang. I didn't normally answer calls from unknown numbers, but the day's events made me think it would be wise to pick up. Sure enough, it was Sheriff Shifflett, and he wondered if I had some time to talk.

"I'm downtown now. Coffee shop in five?" I said with a quick glance at my watch. "My toddler is with his auntie, so I have about fifteen minutes."

"See you in three," the sheriff said, and I picked up my pace as I crossed the street and ducked into the coffee shop across from Spin A Yarn, Mika's store. I ordered my usual late-day beverage – a steamed milk with vanilla syrup – and took a seat by the window with hopes that the late day sun kept me from being visible to Sawyer. He was great with other people . . . until I appeared. Then, it was all Mama all the time.

While I waited, I stared at Mika's shop. It had been her dream to open it ever since we were in college in Pennsylvania, but only after a really hard decade running a preschool did she decide it was time for a change. She moved down from her hometown up north, bought the storefront with the apartment above it in the town I called home, and started her bookstore/yarn shop. It had meant lots of hours of the two of us unloading boxes of used books and shipments of yarn, but I was almost as proud of that store as she was. More, though, I was proud of her. She had taken a risk, and it was paying off.

I took a long sip of my steamer and sat back and inhaled a long, deep breath just as the sheriff walked in. He waved as he headed to the counter for his own order and then made his way over with a giant cup of something coffee-based, so the scent told me.

I smiled, "Thirsty?"

"It's going to be a long night. Normally, I don't do caffeine after three p.m., but today . . . "

"Say no more. For the first eighteen months of my son's life, it was only a late afternoon coffee that got me through to bedtime." I sipped my warm milk and tried to let it soothe the nerves that had suddenly popped up when I saw the sheriff. I didn't know exactly why I was anxious, but I was.

"First, let me assure you that you aren't a suspect."

My blood pressure spiked at the words. "Wait?! What?!"

A smile teased the edge of the sheriff's lips. "Gotcha."

I glared at him until I couldn't hold back my own grin any longer. "You did get me. Too many police dramas, I expect."

"A common problem, which gives me my best gag. You were never a suspect, just to be clear." He chugged half his coffee. "No one who commits a murder first lugs out six cases of Cheerwine." He laughed.

"I'll remember that if I decide to commit a murder and want to throw you off the trail." I felt some of the tension of the day ease with the banter. "But why did you need to see me?"

A certain tightness took hold in the sheriff's jaw again, and my heartrate picked up in response. "We identified the woman in the house."

I took a deep breath. "Okay?"

"You probably know her, actually. Bailey Thomas. Name ring a bell?"

It did, but I couldn't place her. I knew, from funerals, that the bodies of people didn't look much like the people in life, but even with that in mind, I couldn't connect the wispy blonde hair, white skin, and thin frame on the woman in the bedroom with a living face I recognized. "Kind of, but I don't know why."

Shifflett nodded. "She was kind of infamous in town for making trouble, especially at the grocery store. Some people call her, "The 'But the Sign Says' lady."

"OH, HER! Yes, I do know her. Wow." Twice I'd seen her lose it – as in screaming and even throwing things – on a clerk at our local IGA because the price on the register didn't match the price on her item. One time, the high schooler running the checkout had started to cry so hard that the manager had to take over. "She was, um, something," I said as I tried to honor the dead but not lie.

"That's putting it nicely." He cracked his knuckles one by one. "Going to make it harder to catch who did this, I expect."

I let out a long sigh. "Yeah, I guess so," I said quietly, "but how many people would really kill someone over temper tantrums?"

He shrugged. "Hopefully not many."

Now that my surprise at the victim's identity had worn off, I was again trying to puzzle out why the sheriff was telling me all this information. "Can I help somehow?"

"Well, I do have a couple more questions about this morning." He took out a small notebook.

"Shoot." I blushed and wanted to smack my forehead. "Er, sorry, poor choice of words. Ask away." I was pretty sure I'd told him everything I could this morning, but if I could help, I would.

"Did you see anyone else around the store this morning when you were there? Anyone in the woods maybe?"

My heartrate got booming again, but I tried to think, to remember what I'd seen on my way into the building. "Not that I can recall. There definitely weren't any cars there, well, except for the construction equipment." I tilted my chin up and looked at the ceiling as I scanned my memory one last time. "But no, I didn't see any people."

The sheriff made a quick note and then asked, "Anything seem out of place or weird to you as you went through the building?"

"Besides the eerie cookies and the blanket on the sofa that made it seem like people had just walked out, you mean?"

"Well, besides the cookies, yes." He scribbled in his notebook with a little too much attention.

"But the blanket wasn't weird to you?" I said. I was not going to let his careful choice of words go unnoted.

His eyes met mine, and I saw a tinge of color reach the tips of his ears. "Well, yes, but not when we found out Thomas had been living there."

It took me a second to process what he had just said, and then I was still confused. "She was living there? With all that moldy food in the kitchen?"

He shrugged. "Apparently, she didn't care much about that. But by some mistake from the power company, the electricity was still on, and so she had some food in the refrigerator and in the cupboards."

I cringed, and he continued, "Mostly pre-cooked stuff, so she didn't need the oven or stove."

"Still," I said, and then I thought about how this one steamed milk was all I could afford as a "luxury" for at least the next week and wondered if tight finances might have been why Thomas was such a bear at the grocery store. "Do you think she'd been living there long?"

"We're not sure. The electric co-op is going to pull the usage for the past few months. We'll know soon." He sat forward a bit more in his chair. "I know you have to go, but one more question?"

I nodded.

"You didn't, by chance, touch anything around her body when you were there, did you?"

My first instinct was to answer with a quick no, but I knew his question was important, even if I wasn't sure why yet. So I took a breath, walked my way through the memory again, and then said, definitively, "No. I saw she was dead as soon as I got close, and I didn't want to disturb the crime scene." I looked at the sheriff. "And dead bodies creep me out."

"That is, Ms. Sutton, the most honest answer I've ever gotten to that question. Thank you."

I glanced at my phone and saw that it was almost time for Mika to close up shop. I slipped on my coat as I stood, but I couldn't help asking one more question. "Did you think I had touched the body?"

The sheriff stood, too. "No, but since she was still warm when we got there, I was curious if you'd realized that she hadn't been dead long."

A wave of weakness ran up my legs, and I braced myself against the table. "She had just been killed? Like how long?"

The sheriff stared at me for a long minute, and I wondered if he was going to answer my question. But then, he took a deep breath and said, "Thirty minutes before we arrived."

"Oh." I shook the sheriff's hand and tried to act like this information was on par with a report on how long my dishwasher needed to run a cycle as I walked out of the coffee shop. But when I made it past the front window and out of sight of the sheriff, I let out a gasp. That woman was killed while we were there.

3

I took a lap before going to get Sawyer, and by the time I had walked down Main Street, waited at the light, and then back up the road to Mika's store, my heart wasn't racing . . . but my mind was. I couldn't believe I had put us in that much danger.

I knew myself – the only way I was going to calm down was to talk this out, and talking things out was one of the rarest opportunities I had as the single mother of a toddler. He was almost always nearby, and if he was, he was listening. The number of things he'd repeated back to me when I had been sure he had been paying no attention at all was stunning. I was always grateful that I hadn't developed a natural tendency to swear.

That gratitude was magnified when I walked into Mika's shop and saw that Sawyer had turned the showroom into a rainbow spider's web of yarn. I stopped so abruptly that the shop door banged me in the tush, and it was only the sound of scampering feet and Mika's laughter that got me moving again.

There, chasing Saw as a skein of gorgeous magenta yarn unwound behind her, was my best friend, and she looked like she was having the time of her life. Just a few feet ahead of her, my tow-headed guy was yipping with glee as he dodged in and out of the blue, red, and orange strands already crisscrossing the shop. He was playing his favorite game, "Chase me," with the added bonus of yarn.

I made my way carefully to one of the chairs at the front of the store, bending and climbing over strands all the way. Then, I sat down, scrounged out the bottle of white wine that Mika keeps in a small cooler near the chairs at the end of business and poured myself a small glass. I sipped and laughed along with two of the people I loved most in the world until they collapsed onto the floor near me with huge smiles on their faces.

"Well, this looks like it was fun," I said.

"I was having so much fun in Auntie Mickey's store, Mama," Saw said as I handed him a juice box, also supplied from Mika's cooler.

"Oh, I'm glad, Sweet Pea. Ready for some videos?" I glanced over at Mika, and she reached up and behind the cushion of the other chair and drew out a pair of bright-red headphones. "How did you know?"

"The look on your face when you came in and your not-so-stealthy visit with the sheriff across the street." She winked at me, took my iPhone, and plugged in the headphones. "Where do you want to sit, Saw-guy?" she asked.

"Right, there," he said as he pointed behind a tall bookshelf filled with yarn before climbing into the secluded corner with the phone and a thirty-minute time limit of random videos of families from Eastern Europe doing skits with exaggerated facial expressions. Saw loved all those videos, and tonight I was grateful.

As she sat down in the chair across from me, Mika handed me the end of a green skein of yarn and took a blue one for herself. Then, we began to wind the yarn around our fingers, letting the balls of softness form around them. "Okay, so what's up?"

I unspooled the story of the day from our first adventures at the Scruggs store through to Sheriff Shifflett's revelation about how Bailey Thomas had been killed while we were there. Every so often, I had to walk around the store to pull the yarn loose from a corner or from under a table, and each time I did, I saw Mika take a long swig of her wine. Clearly, the story was intense even to hear.

When I finished talking and picked up my third color to begin winding, Mika said, "Holy cow! So how was she killed?"

I dropped my tiny, not-quite-ball of yarn in my lap and looked at her. "Well, I don't know. I didn't think to ask." I finished my glass of wine and shook my head. "Why didn't I ask that question?"

"Right. Why didn't you?"

I glanced over at Saw whose eyes kept getting wider the longer he watched. "I think I was just so flabbergasted that we'd been there when she died, you know?"

Mika looked at the teal yarn in her hand and nodded. "I can see that. But it must not have been a gun shot or anything. You would have heard that, wouldn't you?"

"Unless they used a silencer," I said with mock horror.

"Who do you know in these mountains that has a silencer? Shooting as loudly as possible is practically part of mountain pride around here." She held an imaginary shotgun to her shoulder and fired a round out the front window.

I grinned. "I know. I was teasing. But you're right. I don't think she was shot." I shuddered. "I probably would have seen that, you know."

Mika shook her head a little. "I see what you mean, but let's not think about that. She could have been strangled or poisoned or . . . "

Sawyer was still intent on his videos, but I didn't like talking about all this with him even in the room. In fact, I didn't like talking about it at all. "I expect if the sheriff thought I should know that, he'd have told me. Probably won't have to wait long to find out, though," I said with a nod toward the front window.

Night had fallen outside, but that didn't obscure my stepmother's bouncing step as she came to the shop window, planted her nose against it, and peeked in.

Mika stood up and waved her newly wound ball of yarn. "Come in," she shouted.

My stepmom, Lucille, made everyone happy when she arrived. She was usually wonderfully colorful in both her dress and her personality, and she was always bearing some great cake she'd made. I swear the woman has twenty of those cake carriers I see at the occasional church potluck because she's always leaving them with people and yet somehow always has another on hand.

As she waved and moved around the door into the shop, she seemed particularly cheerful, and I felt my spirits buoy at her presence. While she sometimes gave me straight talk that made me bristle at first when she thought I needed it, she was one of those people who listened well and continued to think about your conversation long after it was done. She was my go-to person when life got hard, and today, well, today felt hard.

"Hey, Women. How's it going?" Lucille asked as she unwrapped her long pink scarf, probably something she picked up in Sri Lanka or India on one of the many trips she'd taken in her life. She then set a cake carrier on the coffee table, removed the top, and revealed a coffee cake that was so thick with crumble that I thought she must have used an entire bottle of cinnamon to make it. Next, she took small paper plates, napkins, and forks from her tote before brandishing a long knife and cutting up the cake and distributing it to Mika and me. She finally pulled a folding chair out from behind my seat, stretched it out, and sat down next to me. "Ooh, that is not the face of a happy woman." She raised her eyebrows as she looked at me.

I glanced over at Sawyer and saw him poke the screen of my phone, the sure signal that the two-minute warning had just flashed up. "I can't really explain now, but it's been a doozy of a day. Call you tonight after bedtime."

Lucille smiled. "Anytime. Now, where's my glass?" She gestured toward the half-empty bottle, and Mika began to pour. "Thank you, Mika. I actually came in to shop if that's okay. I know you're almost closed, but I thought I might see what I could scoop up for Mom out of your bargain bin."

"Of course, Lucille. Please help yourself. Plan to pay only fifty percent of the sale price, though. Ms. Jewel's wine carrier bags sell like hot cakes around here. I'd love to have a few more if she has the time."

Lucille's mother Jewel had just turned ninety-six, and while she wasn't much for walking distances or stairs these days, she still spent her hours crocheting and doing plastic canvas creations for one and all. Her crochet doilies and lace collars were amazing. My forty-six-year-old eyes couldn't even begin to do the detailed work she did.

"Do not tempt me, Mika, and do not tell Mom about that bargain. I'll have to convert the entire spare bedroom for yarn storage," Lucille grinned as she began to rummage through the waist-high basket that Mika used for bargain yarn storage. Within moments, the reusable tote that Lucille had produced from somewhere amongst the folds of her flowing, bright-yellow sundress was full, and she and Mika were headed to the register when I heard Saw's voice say, "Baba!" and was just able to intercept my son before he took his grandmother out at the knees.

"Hey Sawyer Boy," she said as she scooped him into her arms. "So what was it today? Camel sounds or big equipment falling down?"

"No, Baba," Saw said with all seriousness. "Kitties and doggies."

"Ah, yes, I should have known. The end of the day does call for cats and dogs doing silly things, doesn't it?" It's the sign of a good grandmother when she knows about her grandson's YouTube obsessions.

I began to gather the various and sundry things Sawyer had distributed widely around the store as his Baba and his Auntie fawned over him. These two women thought the sun rose and set on that child, and he needed that, especially on the days when my patience ran as thin as rice paper.

My father had married Lucille about five years earlier after a whirlwind affair that began on an online dating site, an entity I was surprised my dad even knew existed. They'd dated three months and then gotten engaged, and then they married the next spring, and given the amount of hand-holding and sweet-talking I saw them do, they were still very much in love with each other . . . which was something my dad deserved more than any man I knew.

When I had shoved all of Sawyer's paraphernalia back in our backpack, I went over to the counter and was met by the exuberant hug of a leaping toddler. My son had yet to learn to warn people before jumping, and I was glad all the people he leapt at with adoration had grown used to impromptu attack hugs or else he probably would have already had his first ER visit. "Oh, thanks, sweet boy. You ready to go home?"

"Yeah, Mama. Bye Baba. Bye Aunt Mickey," he said as he clung to my neck.

I blew a kiss and headed toward the door. "What do you want for dinner, Little Man?"

"Noodles!" he shouted as we headed out to the street, and I heard Lucille and Mika laugh. Sawyer loved "noodles" better than any other food, and I gave thanks for boxed macaroni and cheese again.

. . .

A COUPLE HOURS and five rounds of hide and seek later, Saw was sound asleep, and I was sitting down with a cup of tea and my latest cross-stitch project. But first, I wanted to catch Lucille – and by proxy my dad – up on the day's events. Her phone rang only once, and when she answered, I heard my dad's YouTube videos playing in the background. Like his grandson, he was a fan of the big equipment ones, and videos without dialogue were ideal for him since he was largely deaf. His deafness was also the reason he appreciated me telling Lucille about things instead of calling him directly, well that and he wasn't a chatty guy in general.

When I had finished giving Lucille the run-down, she said, "Well, that's quite a day. You okay?" I felt some of the tension melt away at this question. My dad and Lucille weren't typically the nervous types, but still, what I did sometimes came with risk – mostly of breaking a leg or tetanus – and some people's parents would not look too kindly on it. I thought maybe today would be the day my own would tell me I might need to pursue a less risky career path, but it didn't seem like they would. I was glad because I loved what I did, and I wanted them to be supportive, not anxious.

"I am, I think. It's made me want to learn more, though, but not about the murder. Just about the store. I'm thinking I need to do some research at the historical society."

"Well, tomorrow, my exercise class is at six-thirty, so bring Sawyer over anytime. Baba and Boppy will keep him busy while you research." I could hear her smile through the phone.

"Oh, great. That would be awesome. Plus, you know he loves Baba and Boppy time." My dad had wanted Sawyer to call him Grandaddy, the name us grandkids used for his dad, but somehow, it became Boppy and stuck. It was perfect in the way only an accident can be.

"Paisley, just be careful, okay? Maybe don't tell too many people you were the one to find that woman's body?"

I sighed. Here was the concern I had been expecting. "No worries. I don't plan to. I'm not really interested in being connected to the investigation in any way, certainly not a public way."

"Good," Lucille said. "But what are you going to tell the historical society when you go in?"

I paused. She asked a good question. "Well, everyone around here knows I'm nosy, so maybe I can just tell them I heard about the murder and got curious about the store. Think they'll buy that?"

"Your reputation definitely precedes you, my dear. I think that just might work."

I was still laughing as I hung up. She was right, though. I did need to work on my cover story if I didn't want to answer a bazillion questions about the store and the young woman.

I picked up my current cross-stitch project, Teresa Wentzler's Carousel, and let my mind wander as I blended threads and counted stitches. For four decades now, ever since my mom gave me my first Aida cloth and embroidery floss, I had used cross-stitch as my wind-down in the evenings. I'd sew and sometimes watch TV. Or on nights like tonight when I had a lot to think over, the stitching gave me just enough to focus my attention on while I puzzled through something else.

As I started on the next color – a blend of mauve and brown – I thought about what I needed to find and where I might find it at the historical society. I wanted to look at the society's collection of their own publications because if someone had highlighted old stores or the Scruggs family, I'd probably find some good information. And I wanted to ask about Alice Scruggs in particular. Maybe they had some old news clippings or something. Plus, I knew the society had records of old churches, and the only black church in that part of the county was just down the road from the store. I was hoping I might dig up some information there, too.

As I stitched, I felt my excitement building at the prospect of the historical hunt, but behind that excitement, I could feel something less pleasant . . . and I made a conscious decision to let the trepidation and sadness I felt about the day's events bubble up for the first time. I'd had to learn that as a mother, my son reacted strongly to my emotions, especially the negative ones, and while I didn't want to make my son think it wasn't okay to cry or get angry, I also didn't want him to feel he had to help me cope. I usually just tabled what I was feeling until the evening when I could let loose.

Now, I felt the tears rise up as I thought about that woman, about what her last minutes must have been like. Then, I finally allowed the massive fear that I'd tucked against my spine come up, and I sobbed as I recognized that Sawyer and I, even Beauregard, could have been in real danger this morning.

Only then did it dawn on me that I might still be in danger if the killer had seen me there, and I started to feel panic rising in my chest. I put my sewing hoop down and took a few deep breaths while I stroked Beau's head as he purred against my leg. Then, I took out my phone and called the sheriff's office.

"Sheriff Shifflett," the voice on the other end of the line said.

"Oh, goodness, Sheriff, I didn't think I'd actually get to speak with you. I was going to leave a message." I was all kinds of flustered both by my fear and the surprise of him answering. "Sorry, it's Paisley Sutton. Sorry to bother you."

"No problem, Paisley. I'm the only one here tonight, and with a murderer out there . . ."

I felt my heartrate kick up. "Actually, that's why I called. I just wondered if I needed to be worried for my son and me, I mean since we were there when the killer was . . . and they might have seen . . . and well, I just didn't know."

I wasn't making much sense, but the sheriff seemed to get the gist. "Honestly, I'm not sure. That's why there's a cruiser outside your house right now."

I stood up and walked to the window. Sure enough, right there in the driveway of our farmhouse was a white sedan with the sheriff's insignia on the side. I was glad it was there, especially since I found it really disconcerting that I hadn't heard it pull up. I was still getting used to this house, and I made a note to get a driveway sensor installed asap. "Oh, wow, well, thanks."

"Just doing our job, but I'm sorry we have to do that. I'll keep someone there until we solve the case, as long as you don't object." His voice was kind.

"Oh, no, I really appreciate it. But if you think it's safe, could the officer leave by about seven a.m.? Otherwise, there's going to have to be a demonstration of the siren and the lights, and my neighbors might not appreciate that."

"So noted. I'll have an unmarked car in place before the toddler gets out the door. Got it." He laughed. "Anything else?"

"No, but I am going to write a story about the Scruggs Store for my newsletter unless you think that's a problem for some reason." I hadn't even considered that possibility until I said it, but then, I wondered if stirring up memories might be a problem for the sheriff's investigation.

"Actually," he paused, and I could hear him shuffling papers, "that might just be the thing – if I could ask you to include something in particular. We found a link between our victim and the owners, the Jeffersons."

"The Jeffersons knew Bailey Thomas?" I tried to imagine the sweet older couple who had given me permission to salvage spending time with the raging woman I'd seen in the grocery store those few times, but I couldn't square the image.

"Yes, but not in a good way. She actually was arrested for keying their car." The sheriff's tone had gotten bleak.

"Whoa, why did she do that?" The Jeffersons drove a land-yacht of some sort, a long, blue behemoth of a car. I'd seen it at the restaurant in town where we'd met to talk about my proposal. It wasn't the kind of flashy car that usually drove people to vandalism, or at least it wouldn't drive me to that. I'm more inclined to consider keying the fancy sports car that parks way out in the lot to protect itself. But that's clearly a character flaw on my part.

"Apparently, they parked a little over the line in the library parking lot and ended up taking two spaces." I could practically hear the eye roll in his voice.

"You mean, the huge parking lot that's nearly always almost empty?" Our library was small but wonderful, but the building planners had anticipated the thronging thousands when they paved the field beside it. The lot could easily fit two hundred cars, and I'd never seen more than ten there.

"Exactly. Clearly, she had anger issues. Well, they filed a police report, and she was arrested. They watched her do it, and they gathered witnesses," the sheriff continued.

"She keyed their car for long enough for them to call together people to see it? That's one angry woman." I was trying to picture the scene, a thin blonde woman performing rage-induced vandalism in the very open, very public library parking lot. It was disturbing even in my imagination. But the next thought I had was even more disturbing. "You don't think the Jeffersons killed her do you?"

Shifflett guffawed on the other end of the line. "Now, that would be a sight." He laughed quietly. "No, Berlinda assured me that they were with their daughter."

I sighed with relief. "Okay, good . . . but then, it seems really weird, doesn't it? That she'd die in their house, I mean."

"It seems too odd to be just coincidence, that's for sure." I heard another voice speak in the background, and then the sheriff said, "I have to go, Paisley. But rest assured, you and your son are safe – but write down my cell number just in case, okay?"

I took the pencil that I use to mark off the completed squares on my cross-stitch pattern and scribbled his number at the edge of the sheet. "Thanks, Sheriff." I almost said goodbye, but then I remembered something. "Sorry. Just out of curiosity, did the Jeffersons know that Bailey was living in their store?"

"Oh, well, I didn't ask. But I imagined they'd be shocked. Call if you need anything."

"I will. Thanks." As I hung up, I picked up my stitching. All of this was too weird and unsettling for me to get to sleep easily, so I studied the pattern and went back to it.

4

The next morning, Sawyer was up and at 'em at six forty-five and I rolled out of bed feeling like someone had drained me of blood overnight. When Sawyer turned on every light in the house before I had even put on my slippers, I was able to see, once I pried my eyes open against the bright light, that no vampires were present after all. The French press did have an allure similar to that of the fabled bloodsuckers, so I headed that way.

I put on the kettle and dropped four slices of bacon into the frying pan as Sawyer began one of the few periods of individual play he would undertake for the day. Soon, I'd be wrist-deep in kinetic sand and baby doll hugs, but for now, it was just me, my grogginess, and a gratefulness that my toddler liked bacon as much as I did. Most mornings, it was all he would eat besides chocolate milk and the one blueberry he deemed worthy.

As the goodness fried away in the pan, I thought about our day. Play time and the war of wisdom and wills to get dressed were in order first thing. Then, we'd head over to Dad and Lucille's, where they had a veritable playground of delight in the backyard. In the past six months, they'd bought a swing set, a trampoline, and a kiddie pool that could serve as a hot tub for six on a warm night. Plus, my dad had built Sawyer this amazing contraption for him to climb and swing on, all from reclaimed materials. We had a great yard at the farmhouse, but the fun stuff was at Baba and Boppy's, at least until my budget allowed me to buy a giant swing set.

I was just getting to the part of my thought process where I was planning my order of research at the historical society when a tiny blonde head rammed full force into my rear-end, sending me careening toward the bubbling kettle of hot water.

Fortunately, two and a half years of parenting practice had tightened my reflexes, and I caught myself before we had to call the ambulance. When I turned back to my laughing toddler, my shock must have shown on my face because his round cheeks fell into a frown, and he said, "Sorry, Mama." Then he patted my leg and said, "You okay?"

There was never a calm moment unless this child was sleeping, but those little expressions of kindness were all I needed to do the sometimes-impossible thing of being his mama. He was getting sweeter every day as he came to understand that other people had needs and feelings, and when I didn't want to throttle him, I just wanted to squeeze him.

"I'm okay, buddy. Thanks for saying you're sorry." I reached down and scooped him up.

"What that?" he said as he pointed a still barely chubby finger at the frying pan.

"Ooh, that's bacon." I slid him down to the floor.

"I *do* like bacon," he shouted as he headed toward the couch where Beauregard was snoozing. Fortunately, the cat was wise to his ways and slipped into my room and under the bed before he was snuggled to death.

. . .

THAT MORNING SAW was amenable to pants, so we got to his grandparents without a major meltdown for either of us. Dad was building small birdhouses for a local public garden where he volunteered, so it only took handing Sawyer a drill for him to be so engrossed that he could only manage to say a half-hearted "Bye, Mama" over his shoulder as I left.

The historical society was in the heart of the biggest town in the county, and so I had a bit of a drive ahead of me. I turned on my latest podcast obsession, *Nice White Parents*, and listened to the way people like me, i.e., white parents, often felt they had the right to "save" people of color while also taking over every school their children attended. I was so fascinated by the stories on my newest episode that I barely registered that I'd entered town until I was parking. I'd been here often enough that I was pretty much on autopilot. Still, it was a little disconcerting to realize I had driven all the way there but couldn't remember any of the drive. Another reason to love country living – you can space out on the road without too much risk to yourself or others.

The county historical society was located in an old house that sat next to the early nineteenth-century stone jail. The woman who had owned the house was named Phyllis, and she cooked all the meals for the prisoners and guards alike. Rumor had it that she would torture the prisoners by leaving her cooling pies on the windowsill right beneath their cells and then not bring them pie with dinner. I'd asked the historical society director once if the rumor was true, and she'd assured me that Phyllis was a kind-hearted woman and that pie was served with every evening meal. I decided I liked Phyllis and did my best to unsully her reputation with the locals.

On this Tuesday morning, Phyllis's House, as it was called, was empty save for the lone volunteer, Xzanthia Nicholas, the retired librarian who had guided me toward some of my still-favorite books back when I was in elementary school. Ms.

Nicholas was one of those people who respected anyone who respected her, and since my parents had always taught me to respect my elders, she'd been my guide and my champion for almost four decades now.

This morning, her hair was done in two wide braids that met in a beautiful spiral of gray at the nape of her neck. Long, peacock-feather earrings hung against her brown skin, and she was wearing a draping, aqua dress that reminded me of the ocean on a gray December day. "You look wonderful, Ms. Nicholas," I said as I bent to kiss her cheek. "I love those earrings."

"Thank you, Paisley. My granddaughter makes them for her online store and gives part of her proceeds to a different charity each month. This month, she's saving ferrets, I believe."

I laughed. "I wasn't aware that ferrets needed saving, but I'll be getting a pair of the earrings to help . . . and because they are gorgeous. The feathers came from your birds?"

"You know it. Got to be good for something," she joked. Ms. Nicholas was forever pretending like she didn't love those giant birds like they were her babies. She gave them fresh meal worms twice a day. No one touched those disgusting insects for animals they despised. "What brings you in today?"

"Actually, I was hoping you'd be here because I think you may actually be able to tell me more than the archives, if you have time." I raised my eyebrows with hope.

Ms. Nicholas stood, looked around the tiny house as if bewildered by the throngs of people on hand, and said with a laugh, "I think I can spare a minute. What are we talking about?"

I told her about my desire to write about the Scruggs store in my next newsletter and asked about Alice Scruggs. "I thought people might want to know more about it and about her, you know?"

"You mean you thought the busybodies of Octonia would

go hunting for anything related to the recent murder of that poor woman?" Her face was stern, but I could see a smile at one corner of her mouth. "Why would you ever think that?"

"Lucky guess," I said with a smirk. "Did I ever tell you about the time my dad knew that Tommy McKay was going to ask me on a date before I did?"

She winked. "I do want to hear that story someday. But believe me, I know. Good news, no scratch that, *any* news travels fast around here." She led me up a tiny flight of stairs to the archives room. "Let's start here. I know some things, but it may jar my memory to see what's actually written down."

Back in the day, someone – maybe Ms. Nicholas herself – had begun a system of writing down every key place or name on an index card and then alphabetizing that card in amongst its kindred in an old-fashioned card catalog. It was a painstaking process to add each mention that was discovered in any new materials that were catalogued into the society's collection, but it made finding information so easy. Every time I used the system, I wanted to kiss whoever invented it. On the offchance it had been Ms. Nicholas, I gave her a quick kiss on the cheek when we found a full three inches of index cards on the Scruggs family.

"There's a lot here, Paisley. Where do you want to start?"

"Are these in order by date?"

The harumph from my former librarian told me I had asked a ridiculous question. Of course they were in chronological order. "Let's start with the oldest then."

"Sounds like a plan." She placed two hot pink index cards at either end of the Scruggs cards to mark the place where they'd been removed and then carried the stack to the worktable in the center of the room.

I took out my notebook, and Ms. Nicholas pulled over a second chair. Then, not for the first time, we dug in.

· · ·

Two hours later, we had a clear timeline of the Scruggs family, thanks to the cards, the documents we'd pulled from the collection, and a little help from an online genealogy site. I knew that the store had first opened, as I expected, in the early twentieth century and that it had been a huge deal because it was the only black-owned store in the county. The local paper had done a big story on the grand opening, and that article was full of excitement and enthusiasm. But in that same edition of the paper, the editorials had been full of racist diatribes about people knowing their place and the way the food would be "tainted" there.

That ugliness made me sick to my stomach, and when she saw I was more than a little angry, Ms. Nicholas brought me a bottle of water and said, "Baby, please, those people don't deserve the time it takes you to vomit out their names. Leave them to their ugliness. We've got a story to tell."

I took a swig of the water, carefully put the half-empty bottle on the floor where it couldn't hurt the documents and kept going.

I learned that Alice had run the store herself after her parents died. She had never married, but she'd been in that store at six a.m. every morning except Sunday, when she opened only from three to five for folks in need of something crucial, and had worked that counter until nine p.m. every night.

"I'm tired just reading about what she did," I said as I closed the 1948 yearbook from the black high school in the county. Ms. Scruggs's niece had been the yearbook editor and had dedicated the book to her aunt, "who serves her community faithfully."

"Me, too, but you know, we women have always done what we needed to do." She patted my hand as she stood up. "I'll leave you to look through these last two boxes. Looks like it's photos and clippings. Show me anything interesting that you find?"

"You sure you don't want to go through them with me?" I asked as I stretched and glanced at my phone. Sawyer would just be going down for his nap, so I had a couple more hours.

"Nope. I've got newsletters to address. Just don't hold out on me, okay?" She winked as she walked back to the front parlor.

I lifted the lid off the first archival box and began studying each picture within. All of them were taken by a local black photographer, and most of them were dated from the 1920s to 1950s. Everyone in the images was dressed to the nines with hats and gloves for the ladies, ties and jackets for the men. The photos were mostly posed, families gathered with the wife and mother seated proudly in the center of her clan, two men – clearly brothers – standing with hands on hips as they survey something apparently astounding in the middle distance, a little girl with a parasol standing beside her infant brother.

Most of the images did not have names recorded on them, and so while they were beautiful, they weren't particularly helpful for my research. Still, the catalog had said there was a mention of Alice Scruggs in here, so I kept looking. . . and there, near the bottom of the stack of images, was one of a woman in a casual dress, hair pulled back into two twists at the side of her head, leaning against a post on what was definitely the Scruggs Store front porch.

I smiled as I studied her and then turned the photo over. "Alice Scruggs, Proprietress," someone had written in cursive on the back. I flipped the image back over and studied Alice's face. She was lovely with big eyes and a narrow jaw that was set as steel. A quick glance gave the impression that she was firm, maybe even mean, but when I studied her eyes, I saw a twinkle there, a bit of mischief that made me really wish I had known her.

I snapped a quick photo of the picture with my phone and made a note to ask Ms. Nicholas about obtaining permission to use the photo in my article. As I was enlarging the image on my phone to be sure it was clear enough for me to study as I wrote – I always found that images really helped me solidify what I wanted to say – I noticed something just by Alice's feet. I zoomed in further and then back out, trying to be sure I was seeing what I was seeing.

When I was sure, I set the photo down and sat back in my chair to think. Alice Scruggs wasn't married, at least not under that name. Ms. Nicholas and I had confirmed that. Yet there was clearly a toddler sitting at her feet in that photo. It could easily have been a niece or nephew, of course, maybe a neighbor's child that she kept as a way of making a little extra cash, or even a customer's baby sitting outside while the parent shopped. But something about the way that child was holding onto her legs made me think this was her baby. And a baby born out of wedlock – goodness I hated that phrase – in those days was cause for scandal.

I wasn't interested in stirring up a scandal, for sure, and I really, really didn't want to cast aspersions at another single mother. I had lived with enough judgment from other people in my own life. But there was a story here, and I wanted to follow that trail. The question was how to do that without belittling the strong, confident woman I saw in this photo.

The answer to that question would come in the writing, I expected, and besides, I had come here to see if I could find out more about the first murder in the store, the one that had caused it to shut down. The boxes I'd gone through were all too early, but this last one was labeled: "Murder, May 1999." I took a deep breath and lifted the lid.

Inside, I found newspaper article after newspaper article describing the murder of a man named Luther Angelis. He had been strangled to death behind the counter of the store in broad daylight, and no one had ever been caught. The story made headlines all the way from Roanoke to Richmond, which seemed odd to me especially given the murder rate in Richmond City at the time. But people just don't get murdered by strangers in rural places, I knew this. Our crimes were ones of passion – jilted lovers, angry and drunk friends – but rarely random acts of violence.

Article after article detailed the facts of the day. Angelis had been working at the store as he had for the past five years. He covered the day shifts, running the register, stocking shelves, helping elderly customers by pumping gas. All the people interviewed said he was a nice, quiet guy. Never seemed to give anybody any trouble.

About eleven a.m., a woman came in to pay for her gas and found his body slumped against the cigarette racks behind the counter. The police investigated, but they had no leads. There were no security cameras on site, and the woman didn't see anyone else at the store.

For the next several weeks, the police repeatedly asked the public for information that might lead to an arrest. Eventually, they even offered a reward for that information, but according to a follow-up article published a year after the murder, no arrest had ever been made.

That was all there was to find in the articles, and so I closed up the box and reviewed my notes. The papers made it sound like Angelis, the victim, was just a worker at the store, but everything I'd read about the store had made me think it was still in the family. I opened the genealogy site again and did a search for marriage records for Luther Angelis. Sure enough, there was Luther Angelis, married to a woman named Mary Johnson. On his certificate he listed his mother as Sheila Scruggs.

Another quick search brought up Sheila Scruggs and her marriage certificate to a man named Robert Angelis. The certificate listed her mother as Alice Scruggs and her father as

"Unknown." I would have to confirm at the clerk's office, but it seemed likely that Sheila had left the store to her two children Luther and Berlinda.

I stared at the scribbles on paper before me. All the public records indicated that Alice Scruggs had no children, but here she was with a daughter and two grandchildren. She had a long legacy, and I was so excited to write about it.

But first, I had to figure out how to tastefully address Angelis's murder. I didn't want to hurt Berlinda Jefferson, not after she and her husband had been so kind to me. No wonder the store hadn't reopened after the murder. I couldn't imagine working in a place where my brother was brutally murdered.

The question I pondered next was whether or not there was a connection between Bailey Thomas's murder and Luther Angelis's death. It was possible that it was coincidence that two people were killed in broad daylight in the same rural building, but that would be some coincidence.

And I didn't really believe in coincidences. But I did believe in research, and I clearly had a lot more to do, beginning with a visit to Berlinda Jefferson. I hoped Sawyer was up for a road trip.

After telling Ms. Nicholas about the photo of Alice and asking her to think about what she remembered about Angelis's murder, a request she frowned at but didn't refuse, I walked out into the cool air of the early afternoon. Lucille had texted to say that Sawyer had napped beautifully and was enjoying the trampoline. *Take another hour*, she said. *We'll nap later.*

I smiled. Being an older mom meant that Sawyer had older grandparents, too, and some days, the physicality of a two-year-old was wearing on all of us, but especially my dad. Still, they never balked at watching him, and for that, I was grateful. Today, I was especially grateful for the hour to walk and think and maybe grab a vanilla steamer.

I popped into the coffee shop at the end of Main Street, got my warm milk, and strolled up the sidewalk. The autumn window displays were charming, all pumpkins and scarecrows, and I was tempted to browse for Christmas presents for Mika, Dad, and Lucille. But cash was tight, especially with my latest salvage finds held for evidence, so I just kept walking and let my mind work in the background.

Soon, I found myself at a tiny park just behind the bank in town. A fountain splashed water against bricks, and I planted myself on a bench under a sprawling sycamore to sip and think. I tried to convince myself I was just thinking about my article, about how to feature Alice Scruggs's story in a way that did her justice, highlighted the history of the store, and desensationalized the murders of Angelis and Thomas, but I couldn't get my mind to think logically about those things.

I just kept seeing that child's face leaning against her mother's leg and wondering if she knew what was coming down the train of history for her family.

I HEARD Sawyer's riotous laugh as I parked in front of my dad and stepmom's house, and when I came into the backyard, his Boppy was letting himself get sprayed, head to toe, with the water hose. Saw was cackling with delight at his game, and my dad looked just about as pleased.

When he saw me, my son let the hose go and ran toward me with a shout of "Hi Mama. I got Boppy all wet."

"I see that, Buddy. Is Boppy happy to be all wet?" I asked as I pulled a mostly dry towel off their clothesline and handed it to my dad.

"Ah, it's just water. I'm not made of sugar, you know." He headed inside, presumably for dry clothes, and I helped Sawyer into the trampoline so he could show me his tummy bounce. Then, we went inside, said our goodbyes, and headed back to the farmhouse.

As soon as I unbuckled him from his car seat, Sawyer was off and toward the chicken coop. It was his chore to feed the chickens, but since he was two, that usually involved the work of flinging some ground corn while I slipped behind him and actually put the feed in their feeders. He was an expert at gathering eggs though, if not completely adept at carrying them into the house unbroken.

While the hens pecked around their boy's feet, I cleaned up their "poop boards," ingenious devices that sat under their roosts and were covered in linoleum that made it much easier to keep their coop clean, and pondered what I'd learned about the Scruggs family. I related to Alice Scruggs in so many ways – a working, single mom – but I was a white woman living in the twenty-first century, not a black woman living in the early twentieth century. Those two things alone made a world of difference.

But I had to wonder a little about her life. Maybe she was married. Or maybe the child wasn't hers and I'd read the postures in the photo wrong. Maybe she was a widow. My instincts coupled with the cursory genealogical search I'd done before made me think I was reading that image right, but I always tried to leave room for me to be wrong. At least most of the time.

Eventually, Sawyer tired of picking up tiny shards of corn and letting the hens take them from his fingers, and we headed inside. He found the toy stroller someone had left at the Share Shed at our local dump and proceeded to walk his baby doll around the room while talking to her about how she didn't need to be scared of the Big Bad Wolf.

While the water boiled for spaghetti, I pulled out my "Work Bible," the notebook I used to keep track of *everything* necessary for my work life, and flipped to Berlinda Jefferson's cell number. It was just before five, so I hoped I was calling early enough to avoid interrupting dinner. She picked up on the second ring.

"Hello, Mrs. Jefferson, Paisley Sutton. I hope this isn't a bad time."

"Not at all," she said. "I was actually going to call you. Are you okay?"

I took a moment to appreciate that this woman who had just had someone murdered in her store was asking about me. "I am. I'm fine, but thank you for asking. It was a hard day yesterday." A long deep breath steadied the shudder that went through me as I thought of that poor woman's body. "I'm sorry I didn't call you myself. I figured you probably had enough to worry about."

"Well, we were worried about you most of all, but it was a busy day. I simply can't believe this happened. George was terrified that you had been hurt yourself or had suffered some sort of trauma when you found that poor woman's body." Her voice was strong but shrill, like worry was tightening her vocal cords.

Berlinda's musings made me wonder something, and I jotted a note in my Work Bible. "I drive by there every day, Berlinda, and I never had any idea that someone was living there. No idea at all."

"It's amazing what we don't see when we don't know to look for it," she said with distance in her voice. Then, her tone got clearer, and she said, "But what can I do for you, Paisley, now that I know you're okay?"

"Actually, I was wondering if Sawyer and I could come visit you this week. I found something when I was doing some research, and I'd like to share it with you. I think you'd be interested to see it." I knew I was being obtuse, but I really wanted to surprise her with the photo in person.

"And you're not going to tell me what it is before you come, are you?" I could hear the smile in her voice even through the phone.

"No, ma'am. I hope that's okay. I just really want to see your face when I show it to you."

"I do love a surprise, and if you bring that boy of yours, I'll get a double treat that day. Does Thursday suit? I have a hair appointment tomorrow, and you know us old ladies and our hair." She laughed quietly.

"Thursday is perfect. Wouldn't want to get in the way of you and your stylist. Plus, that'll give me a chance to do a little more research before we come. Does ten work? We'll bring donuts."

"Anytime works if donuts are involved, and ten is great. I'll let George know. I expect he and Sawyer might just be able to get into a little good trouble in his workshop while we talk."

I smiled. "I'll tell Sawyer to pack his hammer."

We said our goodbyes, and I wrote the date in my calendar. It was then that I realized Saw had gone very quiet. Anyone who has spent time with young children knows that quiet is never a good sign.

"Look, Mama, I made you a picture," he said when I found him in the bathroom.

Sure enough, my toddler had painted a lovely blue-green abstract piece on the bathroom mirror . . . in toothpaste. I was just in time to keep him from "cleaning it up" with his tongue.

"Sawyer, dinner's almost ready. You can help me break up the spaghetti." Oh, the things that thrill a toddler.

TWO HOURS LATER, he was sound asleep under his rocket ship sheets, and I picked up the carousel stitching again. My mom had gotten me started on Wentzler's patterns when I was in elementary school. For months, I stitched and stitched on a single carousel horse that had gold highlights on the saddle and headdress. The idea was that it would match my new room, which had lots of gold in it – my favorite color.

It took me more than a year, but I finished the horse. And when I did, my mom took me to a frame shop next to the studio where I had survived one year of ballet to have it framed. The woman at the counter lectured me a bit because I had left the cloth in my sewing hoop for some weeks, and it was hard for her to press out the creases. But when she handed me my carousel horse in a wooden frame with tiny hearts carved in the corners, I was beaming with pride, especially when my mom paid forty dollars, an astronomical sum for our family in the 1980s. Still, just thinking about that gift made me cry. It was a precious affirmation from my mother, and I looked up at the framed golden beauty above my sewing nest. It was still priceless to me.

As I stitched, I thought about Alice and her daughter, Sheila. I wondered what kind of moments they had shared: Hobbies Alice passed down. Lessons she taught. I selfishly hoped that our time with Berlinda would give me some personal insights, not just facts for my article.

THE NEXT MORNING, after feeding Sawyer his morning's quota of two slices of bacon, I put on his favorite movie, *Sharkboy and Lavagirl* and sat down beside him with my laptop. I really tried not to work when Saw and I were hanging out, but sometimes it couldn't be avoided . . . and sometimes we needed to be together but not dependent. This morning's meltdown over the fact that I went to the bathroom without him told me that maybe we needed a little space from each other, even if my sweet boy didn't want me to be out of eyesight.

Fortunately, I'd seen SharkBoy and Lavagirl do their thing at least nine times already, so I was able to provide the requisite responses about the appearance of the spaceship and why Mr.

Electric has those "dog things" without breaking my concentration.

I was trying to put together as comprehensive a family tree as I could online so that I could give it to Berlinda tomorrow. I spent the ninety minutes of the movie pulling records and double-checking them against other records and what I knew of the Scruggs family timeline. And by the time Max's parents were happy-go-lucky again, I had managed to flesh the tree out into about sixty people who went back seven generations.

The oldest generation I had included were Alice's grandparents, people who were almost certainly born into slavery. I wasn't completely certain the two names I had were correct, and I'd tell Berlinda that. But if my educated guesses were right, I might have been recovering a bit of family history that had been lost to that horrible institution.

As the credits ran and Saw began to stir, I closed my laptop and said, "Let's go to a playground." Playgrounds were Sawyer's happy spaces, especially if other children were there and would play with him. I really enjoyed them, too, because they gave my busy guy a place to burn some of his energy while I got to enjoy nature without having to punish my body by being the actual jungle gym.

Plus, Beauregard was always a hit on his leash. That novelty alone drew attention, but mostly, he received a lot of awe because of his size. Children loved his girth and parents liked to try to make witty remarks about how they had toddlers smaller than that cat or how they'd seen a nature show about his kind stalking zebra in Kenya. I tolerated the corny jokes because I needed the interaction with other adults. Single parenting is, I imagine, a lonely endeavor at any age, but in the preschool years, it's downright solitary. I craved conversation, even mundane conversation about shoe sizes and toilet training. If Beau was how I got to talk to adults, so be it.

Still, after chatting with the dad of a four-year-old who had started preschool that fall and was loving it and a conversation with a mom and her nanny about why she only buys organic fruit snacks, I was grateful for a phone call. I stepped to a quiet spot where I could see Sawyer hogging the top of the twisty slide and answered.

It was Sheriff Shifflett. "I hope I'm not bothering you," he said.

"Not at all, but be forewarned. I'm at the playground and may need to drop the phone in the event of an imminent head trauma."

"So noted," he said warmly. "I wanted to let you know, just so you could feel a little more at ease, that Bailey Thomas's cause of death was not a threat to you or your son."

I sucked in my breath. "Well, I should hope not. I mean, I realize that the idea that we might have seen the killer put us in danger, but I didn't know you thought we might have been at risk because of how she died." I tried not to think about guns and knives and things.

"You're right. I'm sorry," the sheriff's voice was strained. "I'm not so good with words sometimes. What I meant is that you were not in any immediate danger that morning. Thomas died from a heroin overdose."

"Oh man, that's sad. Bad drugs or too much?" I had no idea what I was saying. All I knew about drug use I'd learned on television.

"Neither." The sheriff said. "Well, technically too much, but not because she used too much. She wasn't a regular user. Someone injected her to kill her."

I gasped again, both because the idea of killing someone with a drug overdose just felt cruel but also because Sawyer had almost bit it as he made his way down a rope ladder. "That's awful," I whispered once I'd recovered my breath. "But I see what you mean about how we weren't in danger that morning. I wouldn't think a murderer would just have extra heroin to inject random people who saw them there." I tried to laugh, but the idea that someone had been not just committing but following through on the plan for a murder at a place where my son and I were had me a little wobbly.

"Right. Exactly. But that doesn't mean they aren't addled by the fact that you were there when they committed the crime. So we're going to keep the protective watch on for the foreseeable future, okay?"

I nodded and then realized he couldn't see me. "Yes, Okay. Thank you." My heart thumped hard against my chest as I looked around the park to see if anyone was watching me. I wondered if those two parents I'd chatted with earlier were just trying to figure out a way to get rid of someone who was a witness. I tried to peer into car windshields to see if someone was watching us with binoculars. I kept turning and twisting to see around the edges of the playground and into the woods that lined the park around us.

Sawyer was still blissfully playing a game of tag with two new friends he'd met today, but I couldn't get myself to calm down. I was so worked up that the sheriff was practically shouting when he finally got my attention again. "Paisley!" he said. "Listen to me. Do you see the blue Honda at the end of the front row of cars, three cars down from yours?"

I gave my head a little shake and then replayed what he'd just said. "Yes, I see that car."

"Good. Keep watching."

As I stared at the car, Sheriff Shifflett stepped out of the driver's side and gave me a small but very clear nod. "I've got you," he said into the phone.

I smiled and felt a knot rise in my throat. "Thank you," I said. It had been a long time since someone had anticipated my needs, and while I wished my son and I didn't need a police tail, I was touched by his care and confidence. "I hate to tell you this, but the next part of my day is even less exciting." I explained what was up with our plans for the afternoon, and the sheriff assured me that he would be fine with just quietly staying close as we went about our day. I hoped he meant it because in addition to being a bit lonely, exceedingly hard, and beautifully rewarding, parenting a small child was also profoundly boring.

WE PICNICKED AT THE PARK, a guaranteed way to get a full meal in my toddler's belly. I nibbled at my sandwich and fed the rest to Beau. I had wanted to offer Sheriff Shifflett some of the sandwiches I'd packed for us, but I figured if he felt it necessary to stay in his car, he probably didn't want me walking over with my zipper bag of ham and cheese. After Saw finished a half-sandwich, a handful of grapes, and a juice box, I loaded him and our gear into the car and pointed toward home. But as was often the case, we didn't make it there before Sawyer was sound asleep in the back with his neck at an angle that would leave me debilitated for a week. I did my usual route out to Barboursville and then up through Somerset and back West into the Blue Ridge. Every time we took this route, I hoped my son would wake up as we passed the new gas station out by Bacon Hollow because I'd heard their kitchen was phenomenal, but again today, Saw snoozed right on as I drove by, and I had to content myself with the stale pretzels in his snack cup.

The sheriff's blue car putted along at a leisurely distance behind mine. I drove slowly so I could enjoy the mountains and because it was easier to poke along on these winding roads. Plus, today, it seemed wise to stay under the speed limit. I didn't think the sheriff would give a ticket to a person he had under protective custody, but I couldn't be sure.

Four days out of five, I ended up on the road with a sleeping toddler, and while it was exhausting sometimes, I found it was also a great time to think or listen to a book. Today, I had a lot to ponder, so I kept the book off and thought about the events of the last few days.

One thing had become clear from the sheriff's presence at the park today: he and his deputies had not just been sitting outside our house at night. No, we were under constant protection, and while that was comforting on one level, it was also disconcerting that our tiny police force felt it necessary to expend this many resources to protect a mom and her kid. Either they had little else to do – which was a distinct possibility if the crime report in our tiny local paper was accurate – or Sheriff Shifflett was really worried.

Still, there was nothing I could do about what had happened in the past, and dwelling on the hard things of life hadn't ever gotten me anywhere. I pushed my mind to think about something I might be able to figure out, like why someone would have wanted Bailey Thomas killed. I mean, she wasn't a particularly pleasant person. I'd seen that firsthand, and while I tried to give everyone the benefit of the doubt and allow them to behave poorly on a bad day, it seemed that Thomas had nothing but bad days. And she had keyed Berlinda and George's car.

But still, the woman didn't deserve to be murdered. No one did. Yet, she'd obviously done something to someone that made them think killing her was the best option. I could not even imagine being at that point, not even with the people who had caused me a great deal of pain in my life.

One of the things that had served me well as a historian and a salvager was a strong belief that everyone's story was worth telling. To believe that all the time, I had to really work my empathy muscles and do my best to try to understand the whys behind the whats of people's actions. In Thomas's case, I didn't know the specific why of her life, but I knew behind that huffy attitude and mean streak, there was pain. I recognized it in others because I saw it in myself. Pain could make me want to do some awful things, and most of the time, I knew it was but for the grace of God, as the saying goes, that I didn't.

But murder, I just couldn't find my way to understand murder. Maybe I'd learn the why of this one, but I didn't think I wanted to get to a place where I empathized with someone who would do something so awful. Still, I was curious about what Bailey Thomas had done to warrant this end to her life.

As I turned right and entered the crossroads that was Nortonsville, I saw the sheriff's car turn behind me and realized that maybe it wasn't so much what Thomas had done as what she had seen or heard. Maybe she, like me, had been in the wrong place at the wrong time. Maybe she was killed because she was a witness.

A chill went down my spine, and I breathed long and slow as I drove along the Lynch River and made the turn toward my favorite valley, Blackwell's Hollow. All around me the mountains rose up in undulating curves, and the farms of generations spread to their feet. The Episcopal Church stood on a rise with mountains behind it, and I contemplated pulling in to rest my accelerator foot and let the peace of the mountains soothe me a little. But I knew that the minute the car stopped, Sawyer would wake up, and he was on track for a two-hour nap early enough in the day that he'd still be plenty tired come bedtime. I wasn't going to squander that miracle because of an aching ankle.

Plus, out here, someone would notice if two cars pulled into the same parking lot, and there wasn't anywhere else for the sheriff to stop. I drove on down into the hollow and admired the new house going up on the west side of the road. They had done it right – chosen a style of architecture and a location that fit the landscape. The house had a central structure with two wings and mirrored the plantation houses nearby, and it sat on a small hill right in the middle of the valley. The residents would have vistas of the Blue Ridge on every side, and yet, they'd also get the clear sight lines of pasture up close. Pretty perfect.

Another mile down the road, I grinned as I put on my signal and turned onto Shifflett's Mill Road. The sheriff's ancestors had been some of the first settlers here, and their descendants had scattered all around Virginia taking their name and its various spellings with them. I wondered if the sheriff knew which of his distant cousins had built the mill that once operated along this stream.

The drive back north and over the hills to the farmhouse was quiet, and Sawyer only awoke as I crossed the train tracks near our house. He woke up, caught me looking at him in the rearview mirror, grinned and said, "I done sleeping now."

I laughed and picked up the pace toward home. It was a gorgeous afternoon, and that boy had trees to climb.

5

The next morning, after I hauled all our supplies for the day trip out to the car like a pack mule, Sawyer, Beau (who had insisted on coming by jumping onto my back and then perching on Saw's backpack/diaper bag like a raven), and I headed toward Richmond to see Berlinda with a quick stop at the local donut food truck for a dozen of their *huge* glazed. The drive was mostly interstate, my least favorite kind, but it was made tolerable by Sawyer's newfound love of storytelling, which typically involved superhero-like feats of physical prowess performed by himself or Baby, his doll. I kept myself busy by deciphering his grammatically cryptic sentences and marveling at how his brain worked. Still, the drive was tiring, and I looked forward to our meandering return home via backroads in a couple of hours.

We arrived right on time, and Berlinda met us at the door in a velvet track suit, full make-up, and pearls. She looked perfect, and I was glad that I had at least styled my hair into a half-back, half-down number instead of my usual ponytail and that the coffee I'd spilled on myself was hidden under my cardigan. "Come in, you two. Thanks for making the trek to visit us, and look at these," she said as she admired the donuts in their clear-plastic case.

I glanced back to see Beauregard beginning his usual spin before settling into the driver's seat for a nap then smiled at Berlinda as I marveled at her home. The Jeffersons lived in a beautiful brick cottage just up the street from Richmond's carillon, and as we walked in, I heard the bell tower ring out across Maymont Park and the neighborhood at large. It reminded me of the church bells that sometimes rang in our little town, and I felt more at home than I usually did in the city.

Inside, everything was modern and gorgeous. Beautiful vibrant paintings hung on the walls, and the gleaming hardwood floors were adorned with elegant, rich Oriental rugs. The furniture was simple but smart, with lots of rich wood and lush fabric, and the fire was going in a fireplace that was flanked by two built-in bookcases. I wanted to just stay and relax, but instead, I was performing my usual scan to be sure that Saw could not destroy anything.

Berlinda must have seen my visual sweep because she said, "I toddler-proofed a bit. Anything in here is fair game, and if it gets broken, it'll be a memory of our fine visit."

I felt my throat tighten at this kindness. So many people invited us over, but when we came, our visits ended up being stressful for everyone because Sawyer was not a child who could just "touch with his eyes," no matter how hard I tried. That Berlinda had protected not only her things but our time together was a precious gift. "Thank you," I squeaked.

Sawyer was hiding behind my legs, and while I knew he would warm up quickly, I appreciated that Berlinda simply knelt down across the room and said, "Sawyer, it's nice to have you here today. If and when you feel like it, Mr. Jefferson is in the backyard building some benches for our garden. He could always use a helper."

Blonde locks edged out from behind my knees, and then

my son looked up at me and shook his head. "That's fine, Love Bug. We brought some books and toys. You can sit with me for now, okay?"

"You make yourselves at home," Berlinda said with a gesture toward the velour loveseat by one side of the fireplace. "I'll be right back."

I sat down with Saw on my lap and warned him about the fireplace, which had a screen in front of it that looked sturdy but perhaps not Turbo Tot-proof. He nodded and then took out his toy excavator and slid to the floor. When Berlinda returned with a plate of tiny country ham biscuits, donuts, a lidded cup with chocolate milk, and coffee for the adults, I sighed. Hospitality at its finest.

Berlinda poured me a mug of coffee from a silver pitcher, and as I added cream and sugar from the matching set, I said, "Thank you so much for having us over. I just can't wait to show you what I found."

"Well, I hope you'll be able to wait one minute while I inquire, now that I can see you, into how you are. You really are okay?"

Again, I felt myself choking up. "I am. It was a fright for sure." I shot a look at Sawyer, who was busily building a kindling tower on the hearth. "But we are okay." I wanted to say more, to explain about how the sheriff had given us a protective detail, that a car was outside right now keeping watch, but Sawyer understood more than he often let on. I didn't want to scare him.

"Good, I'm glad to hear it." She smiled at me and tilted her head to Sawyer. "Glad to hear you're both well. Now, what is it that you wanted to show me?"

I had been fairly buzzing with excitement about sharing the photo and the family tree with Berlinda, but suddenly, I realized that I was holding the story of someone else's family in my hands, a story she may not know and may not want to know.

I took a deep breath and prayed that I wouldn't hurt her with this information. Then, I reached into my leather messenger bag and took out the copy of the photo that I'd paid the Historical Society to make for me.

As I handed it to her, I said, "This is your grandmother, Alice Scruggs, on the porch of your store."

Berlinda's hand flew to her mouth as she studied the photo. "Grandma Alice. Oh my. I've never seen a picture of her before."

A wave of relief flooded through me. Berlinda had called her Grandma, which meant she knew of her before this. "No pictures at all?" I asked both out of curiosity and to mask my relief.

"Well, not when she was this young at least. She looks just like my mother." Berlinda pulled the image closer to her face and said, "Wait! Is that Mother?"

I watched as Berlinda's face flushed and tears sprang to her eyes as she looked up at me. "They're at the store. That's the front porch of the store."

I nodded, too emotional myself to speak.

Her gaze returned to the photo. "Mom never talked about her childhood much, but she did talk about her mom, my grandmother."

My breath caught, and I cleared my throat. "If you don't mind me asking, I'd love to hear about what she remembered."

"Oh, I'd love to tell you, have you include it in your article if you want. I want everyone to remember these two amazing women." Berlinda's eyes shone as she spoke, and I understood at least a bit of what she was feeling. Everyone wants to know their story matters. Everyone wants to be heard.

I took out my notebook and was just about to write the date at the top when Sawyer stepped to my shoulder and whispered, "I want to help make bench."

I looked up at Berlinda to be sure she'd heard, and she smiled widely.

"Oh, good, Mr. Jefferson needs help. Maybe your mom and I can talk out there. He has a fire going in the firepit by his shop, so we'll be warm." Berlinda stood.

I smiled. Sawyer wasn't going to go anywhere without me, and I appreciated that Berlinda realized that. But I was also glad Saw would be distracted since I needed to focus and since the conversation might not be really appropriate for toddler ears.

Sawyer and I followed Berlinda into the backyard after putting on our coats, and when I saw the comfy chairs under a pergola with a warm fire glowing in the middle of a stone hearth, I grinned. This was a treat for both Sawyer and me.

"Well, hello young man. Would you be willing to help me make some holes in this piece of wood?" George boomed as he saw Sawyer approach. Mr. Jefferson was a big man, six foot four at least and broad in the shoulder. In contrast to his slim, petite wife, he looked massive, but he also sported a long white beard against his dark skin, and with his suspenders and red shirt, he looked downright jovial.

"Mama," Sawyer said as his chubby cheeks flushed with delight. "Santa Claus needs my help."

Berlinda grinned. "Yes, he does, Sawyer. And Mama and I will be right here if you need her, okay?"

Sawyer looked at me for one last second and then turned toward Santa and held out his hands. "I use drill," he said.

"Well, sir, I guess you will since you know your tools." George looked at me and winked.

I turned to Berlinda. "He builds a lot with his Boppy, and while Boppy is awesome, he's no Santa Claus." I laughed.

"George cultivates that impression from about September until January. He even plays Santa Claus at the local bookstore some years. Loves it." Berlinda picked the photograph back up and said, "Okay, now tell me about this photo of Mother and Grandma Alice."

I filled Berlinda in on where I'd found the image and then gave her the printout I'd made of her family tree. Her eyes roved over the page when I handed it to her, and then she met my gaze. "Paisley, you have outdone yourself. Thank you. I recognize many of these names from Mom's stories about Grandma's family, but I've never been able to make sense of how we are all kin." She held up the paper. "This is a precious thing you've made here."

"Oh, I'm so glad you think so. I didn't want to seem like I was intruding on your family history. But I know that sometimes people don't know how Uncle So-and-So is actually an uncle." I smiled.

"And for African Americans, it's even harder because we don't know much beyond a few generations back. You've leaped the wall as my genealogist friends say, and we can maybe find where our people were enslaved. Thank you, Paisley."

I blushed and said, "Really, it was a small thing for the gift you gave me of being able to visit your store before it was torn down." I sighed. "How are you with that?"

Berlinda sat back in her chair and propped her feet on the edge of the firepit. "It's sad, really, but also necessary. The building is in terrible shape, and after Luther was killed there, I just couldn't figure a way for us to reopen. It would just be so expensive, and I would want to be sure we did it well to honor Luther and the history of the building." She shook her head. "All tragedy. All of it."

I sighed. "I read the newspaper articles about Luther's death. I'm so sorry. How horrible that must have been and then for them not to have caught the person who killed him."

Berlinda sighed. "It was awful and so strange. Luther never had an enemy that I knew of. He was one of those people who was simply sweet and kind. He didn't gossip, didn't get into trouble, didn't even much like to spend time with people except at the store. He read books and cooked the best venison stew you ever ate. He was a simple man, my brother. It still doesn't make any sense to me why someone would kill him."

I shook my head. "He sounds like he was a wonderful man."

"He was. We were really close as kids. Our daddy died when we were young, car accident, and it was just us and Mother. The three of us were thick as thieves, even though Mom taught school and also supervised the help at the store." She looked at the picture of her mom and grandmother again. "I always wished we'd lived in that house growing up. It seemed so fancy to be able to go grab a soda whenever you wanted."

"Oh, you didn't live there?"

"No, Mother believed it was better for us to live in town, closer to the school so that she could keep an eye on us. Plus, we needed the money she got from renting out the house behind the store to one of her employees." Berlinda smiled. "It was always some nice, young man who just needed a little help to get his footing in the world. I think Mother imagined I'd marry one of those young men one day and take over the store. I wasn't interested, though. I had it in mind to go to college already, and it didn't suit me to live a life tied to that place, as much as I loved it."

I nodded. I saw how hard Mika worked to run her store, how she couldn't afford employees and so this meant she always had to be there. Mika loved it, but she was a woman in her forties. I could totally understand why a young woman wouldn't think much of that life.

Berlinda held up the family tree I'd made. "Could I ask you to correct something here? Our Daddy's name was Roger Angelis, not Robert."

"Of course," I said. "I'm sorry I got it wrong. That's how his name was listed on Luther's marriage certificate."

Berlinda shook her head. "That's because that wife of his flubbed it up. She wooed my brother right into stupid."

I loved that expression, but quashed my smile when I looked at Berlinda's frown. "So she filled out the marriage certificate?"

"I expect so. She did everything for him, treated him like he was an imbecile." I could see a rise of red coming up over the collar of Berlinda's sweatshirt. "I never did understand what Luther saw in her."

I thought of the cookies on the kitchen counter in their house, of the little boy's room in the back. "Do you keep up with Luther's son?"

Berlinda snapped her head in my direction like a startled bird. "You know about Henry?"

"No, I mean, I saw his clothes in the house and assumed he was Luther's son."

Berlinda's fingers were twisting the napkin on her lap into a tight tube. "He is. And no, we don't." Her tone was tight and her expression guarded for the first time during our visit.

I quickly changed tack. "Did they investigate Mary for Luther's murder?

Berlinda broke the stare she was holding on the fire and looked at me. "Oh, yeah, we wondered about that, too, when he died, but the police said she had an alibi. She was a suspect for a time, though."

"Do you mind if I look into her a little, just for my story? I won't include her, but I find that researching everything I can helps me tell a more robust story, even if I don't tell it all." I was telling the truth, but I also wondered if twenty years ago the police might have missed something about Luther's murder. I didn't need to worry Berlinda with that idea, though.

"Sure. You've got her name right here, Mary Johnson. She grew up over in the Valley, I believe. Elkton or somewhere."

"You haven't talked to her in a while then."

"Tried not to talk to her even when she was married to my brother. So no. Not a peep in over twenty years, which is fine by me." Berlinda stared out across their garden, and I took that as a sign that this part of our conversation was over, which was fine by me.

I glanced at my phone, eleven-fifteen. Sawyer was going to pass the tipping point from adorable to tantrum in about fifteen minutes, so I knew I needed to ask the hard question I had. I took a deep breath and just went for it. "Berlinda, I'm sorry to have to ask this, but do you know who your grandfather was, your mother's father?" I rushed on. "I ask because I couldn't find any records about him, and I wondered if your mom knew him at all. Wondered if he and your grandmother were married, if he worked at the store with her? I mean, clearly, I have no problem with a woman being a mother on her own, but in that day –"

Berlinda interrupted me and smiled. "She wasn't married, not that I know of. And I imagine that was hard for her. I don't know the exact circumstances of my mother's birth, but I do know there was a secret there. The story was too painful for Mother, so I didn't press much when I was old enough to understand it hurt her to talk about it. But I have always been curious."

I sat back and took another deep breath before I asked my next question. "Would it be alright with you if I did a little research into that, too? See if I could maybe figure out who your grandfather was and the story behind his relationship with your grandmother?" I tilted my head and raised my eyebrows. "Please tell me to mind my own business if you'd like."

Berlinda leaned forward and took my hand. "Paisley Sutton, if we didn't trust you with our stories, we would never have let you in our store. I appreciate you asking, but there is nothing there that you can turn up that will surprise me or hurt me.

Whoever that man was and however he came to be my grandfather, I am grateful because, well, here I am."

"Thank you," I said as I squeezed her hand. "One more hard question, and then I'm done, I promise."

"Your questions aren't hard, Paisley. Just honest. I like honest. Ask away."

"Any idea who might have killed Bailey Thomas or why she was living in your store?" I winced, hoping I hadn't gone too far with my nosiness.

"Not a clue on your first question, but the second one is easy. She was living there because I told her she could."

I sat back hard against the Adirondack chair. "You told the woman who keyed your car that she could live in your store? Why?"

"Because she needed a place to live, and the house was sturdy and available." Berlinda said it so matter-of-factly that it took my brain a minute to realize that her generosity was so natural that she thought nothing of it.

"Wow. That's mighty generous."

Berlinda shrugged. "I'd have wanted someone to do the same for me. George was a little hesitant. A single woman alone in an old building, I guess, but it's technically my building so." She took a long breath. "I hope that place gave her a little peace in her last days.

I sighed. "I'm sure it did. Does the sheriff know that?" I asked.

"He does. I told him the day he called. Figured it was important for him and others to realize she wasn't squatting or some such. She was just down on her luck and needed a place to stay."

I shook my head. "Berlinda, you are something else. Thank you for your time, and thanks again for allowing me to salvage a few things from your store. I'll send photos of what I found over to you when I get it back from the police. It's evidence."

"Well, that's kind of you, Paisley, but whatever you find is yours to keep. We conducted business, and anything I needed from that place I took years ago. But I would love to see the pictures just so I can see what you do with this salvage business of yours. I love that you make treasure out of what might have become trash."

I grinned and stood up. "Have they rescheduled the demolition of the store yet?"

"Not yet. My understanding is they have to close the case or have it under investigation for a time at least before they can take down the crime scene." She shrugged as she stood up. "It's been falling down for ten years. It can wait a while longer."

Sawyer barreled into me and held up a small figurine. "Santa George made me a little man," he said. Sure enough, the figurine was a miniature version of Santa George himself.

"Thank you," I said as George walked over. "He'll treasure that."

"And I'll treasure this," George said as he waved to a small bench on the ground. Up and down the legs were small drill marks that looked a lot like woodpecker holes. "It's one of a kind, and it's going to be perfect on the other side of that fire." He carried the bench over, put it down, and sat on it. "Sturdy as a rock. Thank you, Sawyer. You are a fine assistant."

"I made that bench with Santa," he said to me as he held onto my leg.

Berlinda put her chestnut fingers in my son's blonde hair and said, "Yes, sir, you did. Well done."

WE HAD BARELY MADE it out of the city center when Sawyer fell asleep, and I put on Over the Rhine's *Ohio* album as I wandered west across the state. Their music had a way of settling into and over me so that I could think, and the conversation with Berlinda had definitely given me a lot to think about. First there was Luther's wife, who sounded like a real gem and who definitely had some motive to kill him, if petty anger was motivation enough. I was a little bit inclined to do a little digging into Angelis's murder, but I had enough questions about the store itself without putting my nose where it didn't belong.

Then, there was the question of who Sheila's father and Berlinda's grandfather was. I wanted to focus most of my attention on seeing if I could discover his identity, but I really had no idea how to go about doing that. I was hoping that Dad and Lucille might have some ideas given how long they'd lived in Octonia. Maybe they had some guesses. Or maybe they'd have some suggestions about who I could ask, discreetly, about their guesses.

But for most of the ride, I pondered the fact that Berlinda had let a woman who had vandalized their personal property live in a building they owned. It seemed impossible to me to be that generous – that generous and that wise. After all, they hadn't gone in and cleaned up the place. I thought it was a sound choice to tell someone they could have a dry place to live but not to go so far as to make that place perfect. I probably would have made the mistake of cleaning up the place, and from the looks of things, that effort would have been wasted on Bailey Thomas. If she couldn't be bothered to throw away molding cookies . . . I shook my head.

Still, she'd been there with Berlinda's permission, so that meant whoever killed her knew she was living there. I tried to think back to what I'd seen in the house, but nothing came to mind that made me think someone else was staying there with her. The boy Henry's bedroom had seemed like it was just as he left it on the day his father was killed, and I hadn't noticed any suitcases or anything in the other bedroom. But then, I had beat a pretty hasty retreat once I'd found Thomas's body, so maybe I'd missed something.

But if I was right, someone came to that house with the

intention of killing her, which seemed to back up what the sheriff had said about someone bringing heroin along for that purpose. Someone was very determined to end Thomas's life, and I was hoping the killer had more of a reason than just being held up in the grocery store line. Sadly, Thomas's own behavior seemed to demonstrate that even small slights could bring up the biggest rages.

Sawyer must have been exhausted from his bench-building escapades because he was still sound asleep when we crossed Highway 29 close to town. He would probably wake soon, but I figured I had enough time to just drive by the Scruggs store. I was hoping that seeing the place again would jar something else loose in my mind, remind me of something I had thought was incidental.

As I turned toward the mountains, my phone rang, and I snatched it out of the console before the ringtone could wake the sleeping toddler. "Hello," I whispered into the mouthpiece.

"Paisley?"

"Yes, it's me. My son is sleeping. What can I do for you?"

"Oh, sorry. Hope I didn't wake him," the woman on the line said. "I'm calling from the sheriff's office. Sheriff Shifflett wanted me to let you know that you can come pick up most of your salvaged items from the Scruggs store. They've been cleared from evidence."

I was surprised. I thought maybe it would be months before I'd get those things back. "Wow, that's fast."

"The sheriff made a judgment call that the items you'd gotten from the store were technically in another building from the murder and so didn't need to be held. It'll be a bit longer for the clothes and such, though." I could hear her shuffling paper in the background.

"Okay, where do I come?" She gave me the address of the evidence locker in a building downtown, and after I hung up, I immediately started trying to figure out when Saw and I could pick everything up.

He was beginning to stir, so I picked up the pace and slid Beauregard back further in the front seat, an action which got me quite the glare. "I just didn't want you slamming into the dashboard, boy," I said as I scratched his chin. He continued to glower at me.

I began to slow on the last curve before the store, and since Sawyer was bound to wake up anyway, I put on my turn signal to move into the parking lot. But before I actually turned, I saw a big Dodge Ram pickup in the small, gravel lot. Sometimes people stopped to answer calls or, like me, fish binkies out from under the car seat, so at first I thought nothing of it. Then, I saw the large, white guy with a big red beard on the front porch.

He was peering in the windows of the store, and as I slowed further, I saw he had a crowbar in his left hand. Just as my tires started to growl against the gravel, I changed course and pulled back on the road. I tried to keep my speed steady, make it look like I'd just mis-steered a little, and drove on down the road. I had no idea what the man was doing, but I did not think it in my best interest for him to see me.

A bit further down the road, when my cell service picked back up, I dialed the sheriff's office. The sheriff got on the line immediately, and when I told him about the man, he said, "Paisley, drive out to 29 and go to the big red gas station. I'll meet you there."

I sighed, glanced at the toddler who had miraculously dropped off to sleep again, and went to flip my turn signal to turn left back to the main road. It was only then that I realized I'd had my right-turn signal on this whole time. If that man had looked, he would have known I was headed to the store.

Startled, I took the left too fast and felt the cat and everything else shift hard to the right. I overcompensated for my error by slamming down on the brake, and I heard all of Saw's toys, a month's supply of juice cups, and something heavy and solid slide forward into the passenger's floor pan. I looked back to see Sawyer, somehow, still asleep, and then I glanced over to see a wooden box just below Beau's gray feet. "Shoot," I whispered. "The jewelry box from the store."

I had forgotten all about it, and now, I had stolen it . . . if my heart hadn't been racing from seeing the man at the store and thinking he had probably seen me, it would have been at the thought that I might be charged with theft. But as I drove the few miles to the gas station, I took some long, deep breaths and resolved just to explain the situation to the sheriff and take the next step after that.

When I pulled into the station, I saw the sheriff's marked cruiser immediately and pulled up next to it. A gold sedan pulled up on my other side, and only then did I realize this was the unmarked car that had been following me all day. I purposely relaxed my shoulders and reminded myself that we were safe, and then I woke up Sawyer, gave him my phone with videos on it, and stepped out into the parking lot, jewelry box in hand.

"Are you okay, Paisley?" The sheriff asked as he came around his car to lean against mine. "You sounded a little nervous on the phone."

I sighed. "I was nervous, but honestly, I'm not sure why. I don't even know if the man saw me." I took another deep breath. "I think this whole situation has just got me a little worked up."

The sheriff nodded and then waved his waiting deputy over. "You got a description of the guy?"

The young man nodded. "White, about six foot two with red hair and a long beard. Blue jeans with a green flannel shirt and brown work boots."

"Good. Did you notice anything else about him, Paisley?"

I looked from one officer to the other and said, "Just the crowbar."

The deputy made a note in his phone. "I didn't see that. Thanks," he said.

"Was he using the crowbar?" the sheriff asked me.

"No, it was just in his hand. Hanging there." I glanced at Saw in the car behind me and lowered my voice. "But most people don't walk around with crowbars, right?"

"Right," the sheriff said. Then he turned back to the deputy. "Let's get the word out about this guy, and why don't you join the patrol car that's there. Just in case."

The deputy nodded at his instructions and went back to his car.

"Gracious. The poor Jeffersons. All this and then someone breaking into their store," I said.

"It's a good thing you were driving by . . . but I have to ask, why were you driving by?" Sheriff Shifflett's expression smiled, but he also held my gaze while he waited for my answer.

"Honestly, I just wanted to see the building. Places really help me understand stories, and well, I just wanted to see this one up close again." I explained about our visit to the Jeffersons that morning and how I was writing an article about their family and the store. "So I just wanted to share the air with the building for a few minutes."

The sheriff listened intently and nodded along until I was finished with my long-winded explanation before he said, "Okay. Well, that all makes sense, and like I said, it was good you were going by. Now, I probably don't have to say this, but that is still an active crime scene."

I nodded. "I know. I wouldn't have gone in. And I won't." I felt a flush rising in my cheeks. "Please know that I want whoever did this caught, and I wouldn't risk that in any way." I looked down at the jewelry box in my hands.

"What's that?" Shifflett said as he followed my gaze.

"Well, this is really embarrassing, but I need to give this to you." I held out the box as I explained that I'd put the box in my car during my visit earlier in the week and had forgotten about it in the midst of everything. "It happened to slide out from under my seat when I was coming to meet you." I realized how weirdly coincidental this sounded, but I was telling the truth . . . and I had to trust the truth.

Sheriff Shifflett studied the box in my hands and then looked at my face again. "Well, I guess we should see what's inside."

I gasped. "We can do that? Isn't this evidence?"

"It is," he said as he pulled gloves out of his back pocket. "I'll take a picture so we know what it looks like, and we'll replace anything we find. Just a quick look."

Carefully, he took the box from me, set it on the hood of my car, and opened the latch. I leaned over to look inside and saw the sparkle of rings and bracelets. I knew nothing about jewelry, but I found it hard to imagine that people would put a jumble of real diamonds and gemstones into the mess that I saw inside. Everything was tangled. The sheriff snapped a quick picture with his phone, but when he tried to lift a single bracelet, everything in the box came with it.

"What a mess," he said as he tried to free one or two pieces from the mass of sparkles. "Looks like most of it is costume jewelry, but I'll get it looked at to be sure. Where did you find this?"

"On the top shelf of the closet in the bedroom where I found the body." I held my tongue even though I wanted to explain, again, how I'd forgotten to mention the box earlier.

The sheriff nodded as he turned the jumble of jewelry around and around again. "Looks like someone put this project away for another day."

I nodded. "That's what I do . . . put things away until Sawyer is older and I'll have more time to sort them out.

Fixing broken jewelry, jigsaw puzzles, and a clean car are all on hold."

The sheriff chuckled as he moved to put the ball of jewelry back in the box. "Hmm, there is one more thing." He picked up an old-fashioned door key. It had a scrolled top and the bit was ornate with two teeth, each carved in geometric shapes. It looked like hundreds of keys I'd found in my salvage work. I sold them for three dollars apiece on my website, and jewelers bought them all the time to make pendants or interesting rings.

I leaned forward to study the object. "That looks like a skeleton key," I said. "It could be valuable."

The sheriff took another pair of gloves from his pocket and handed it to me. "You're the expert. I'd probably end up calling you to evaluate this anyway."

I smiled as I slipped on the gloves and then took the key from his hands. It was heavy, and at the top, I could see that an elaborate filigree had been pressed into the metal. I studied the barrel, looking to see if there were any words, but I didn't see any, which meant I couldn't specifically identify what the key was for. "It's old. Maybe nineteenth century, and it will probably open a lot of things. I imagine it was for the doors in the house, but it could have been for something else."

"Something like a safe?"

I looked at the key closely again. "Maybe? But it looks more like it's for something larger. Could be a cabinet or a dresser."

"Did you see anything in there that might have matched this key?" Shifflett gestured over his shoulder toward where the store sat over the hills.

I leaned back against the car and tried to remember my walk through the store and the house, but nothing came to mind. "I don't think so, but I wasn't really looking with that idea in mind. Anything that big would have been beyond my ability to take out that day."

"So you're saying you're not the Salvage Dawgs?"

"I wish," I said with a chuckle. "But I don't come with a crew and a crane typically. I can't carry out big items, so I don't really pay attention." I took a deep breath as I prepared to ask my next question. "But if you wanted me to walk through again ... "

"Let's do it. Can you go now?" He was moving toward his car.

"I can, but it will mean my son has to be in the car even longer. He's patient with me, but I may be testing his limits. Give me thirty minutes to leave him with my friend, and I'll meet you there?"

"Sounds good. Just wait outside when you get there." He looked at me firmly.

"Of course," I said and tried not to be annoyed.

SAWYER WAS reticent about our change in plans, and I couldn't really blame him. I didn't like shifts in my day's outlook either. But he warmed quickly to the idea of visiting Auntie Mickey's shop when I reminded him that she had "hot chocolate milk."

And Mika was, as usual, totally happy to have a two-year-old running wild in her store. "Keeps me young," she said.

"Funny, I feel ancient after a day with him myself," I answered with a chuckle. "See you soon, and thanks."

I left my son gamboling about her store like a chubby-cheeked elf and tried to work up some modicum of excitement about going back into the Scruggs store after I texted the sheriff to let him know I was on my way. Normally, I felt about trips to old buildings like I had about going to Kings Dominion Amusement Park as a kid ... I was all bouncy and couldn't wait to get there. But finding a dead woman, well, that had damp-ened my spirits.

Still, I was eager to see if there was something that fit that key. People didn't normally keep old keys in particular boxes if they were unimportant. Most of the time, I found piles of old

keys in the junk drawers of kitchens or in a custodian's locker in
an industrial space. People, me included, were loath to throw
out keys just in case, so we tossed them in with rubber bands
and old batteries and dug them out when we found our old
suitcase locks from 1987.

But someone had cared enough to put this one in this
particular box. Given, the jewelry in there wasn't well-cared-for,
but as the sheriff had suggested, maybe someone was just
waiting for a time when she'd have a quiet hour to focus and
untangle that mess. Goodness knows, I was looking forward to
those hours when Saw was a bit older, and I had more time to
concentrate.

When I pulled up to the store, the sheriff was there, as was
the deputy I'd seen at the gas station, his car parked prominently right by the side of the road. They were deep in conversation, so I took my time pulling together my salvage kit that
Sawyer had strewn across the backseat. My mammoth Maglite
was underneath his fox backpack, and my own mini-crowbar
was wedged beneath his car seat. I found my fabric gloves,
which I kept for handling paper or photographs, glued together
by raisins, and my small tool kit with screwdriver and hammer
was behind the rear seat and wrapped around the handles of
my reusable shopping bags. Someday, along with an hour to
think, I was looking forward to driving a clean car again.

By the time I had placed everything back in the black, soft-
sided tool bag my dad had given me, Sheriff Shifflett was at the
front of the store. I waved, tried to be sure I didn't have old
Goldfish stuck to my pants, and headed over. "Where do you
want to start?" I asked.

"I guess we begin in the store, unless you think that's a
waste of time. You're the expert, remember?" He took off his hat
and looked at me.

"Oh, well, then, to be thorough, I think we should check
there." I started through the door, determined to look like an

expert even though I felt like anything but. "Did you come through here the other day?"

"I did, but just for long enough to see that it would take a real feat to get to the house through here."

"You got that right," I said. "I had to belly-crawl . . . " I trailed off when I saw the sheriff's expression: half-shock, half-respect.

"You crawled through there?" He gestured toward the tiny corridor that led to the back of the house. "With your young son waiting in the car?"

"I had let a friend know that if she didn't hear from me to come get Sawyer." I felt myself blushing again. It was hard being a single parent, and the choices I made to keep us all well came with some calculated risks, risks I really did consider before I took them. But the fact that I knew that never seemed to lift the shame I felt when people questioned my choices. "We can just go around," I muttered in an attempt to change the subject. "I don't see anything in here that would fit that key." I swung my flashlight in one more arc around the room and then went back to the front door.

The sheriff followed me to the house's exterior door, and I opened it carefully. I knew Bailey Thomas's body was gone, but still, she had died in this place. I wanted to respect that.

Inside the kitchen, everything looked the same. Same moldy cookies. Same 1970s Formica. But nothing that looked like it would go with that key. I waved my light toward the living room and headed that way.

Again, nothing had moved, but this time, I noticed a tall, wooden pie safe in the front corner of the room near its only window. The piece of furniture stood about shoulder-height to me and was fronted with punched tin. It looked pretty rustic at first glance, as one might expect from a primitive piece of furniture in a rural home, but when I checked out the legs, I saw they were turned to curling feet, not just the sanded square legs I would have expected.

I ran my flashlight up the front of the safe, and sure enough, there was a keyhole right above the two knob handles. Typically, pie safes were handmade with wooden toggles that spun to keep the doors shut. People kept food in them – pies, yes, but also bread or fruit or anything you didn't want bugs or mice to get. But I had never seen one with a lock. Food was often precious up in these mountains, but still, most people didn't lock it up, not like this.

"Can I see the key?" I asked as I put my hand behind me. The sheriff took out a small evidence bag and then placed the key in my hands. "Thanks."

I slid the key into the hole and turned. It slid like oil over glass, and I heard the tumbler inside clunk over. All of me wanted to reach up, pull one of the knobs, and open those doors to see what treasure awaited, but I knew this was not my job. I stood up and stepped back.

Sheriff Shifflett didn't hesitate, and when he opened the door, we both had to lean in to understand what we were seeing. It took my eyes a minute, but then I realized that what I was looking at was stacks and stacks of cold, hard cash.

6

"So then, he asked me to leave, thanked me for my expert services, and escorted me to my car." I was still processing what I'd seen at the Scruggs store when I picked up Sawyer from Mika's shop. "I mean, Miks, I have never seen that much cash in my life."

"Did you see the denominations on the bills? Are we talking ones or hundreds here?"

I shook my head. "It was dark, so I couldn't say for sure. But thousands of dollars even if it was small bills. And just right there in that abandoned building all this time."

Mika stood up and began gathering the balls of yarn she had wound while Sawyer had played. Now, he was contentedly eating an orange and trying to toss stitch markers into a basket that Mika had set up as an impromptu basketball goal.

"And before that, even, it was just there in the living room. I've heard of women squirreling away money in cookie jars and coffee cans, but thousands of dollars in a pie safe. Didn't the Angelis's use a bank?"

I shrugged. "The piece of furniture was weird, too. It clearly was old, late nineteenth century, I'd say. But I don't think it was originally a pie safe. Maybe it had been a wardrobe at one point and then was converted into a pie safe. The lock and the legs just didn't make sense on a traditional primitive piece." I cast my mind over all the books on antiques I'd read over the years and thought of all the furniture I'd seen in shops and attics all over the Blue Ridge. But I'd never seen anything like this.

"Are you thinking someone turned that piece into a humbler looking one just so they could hide money in it?" Mika asked as she scooped up Sawyer with one arm while dropping the balls of yarn in his basket with the other.

"I don't know what I'm thinking," I said. "It was just weird."

"It was just weird," Saw mimicked.

"It was, Little Man. But are you ready to go? Chicken nuggets and noodles for dinner tonight."

"Chicken nuggets yucky," he said with deep disdain.

"Oh yeah?" I asked as I gathered our things, took Saw's hand and headed toward the car. "Yesterday, you loved them. But not today, huh?"

"Nope. Yucky." I sighed as I strapped him into his car seat. Toddlers were fickle, but at least they were predictable in that. More predictable than stacks of money in a pie safe.

THAT NIGHT, as I picked up my cross-stitch and sipped my vanilla chamomile tea, I thought more about that piece of furniture. I was no expert, by any means, but it really seemed unlikely to me that a cabinet of that quality would have had rough-cut, punched tin on it originally.

I blended a light beige and a light tan thread together for my next stitches, gave thanks for my magnifier and light, and wondered if the sheriff had taken the entire piece with him when he collected the cash. I decided to take advantage of having his cell phone number and text to ask.

No emergency, but did you take the pie safe in as evidence?

His reply was almost immediate. *Sure did. Want to get a look at it in better light?*

I do. Tomorrow at ten? I felt a little bold suggesting a time, but Sawyer had a rock-climbing class with Lucille then, and I knew I could get away for a bit.

Sounds good. You can pick up your other items then, too? Maybe we can get coffee as well.

I blushed and then immediately felt stupid. He wanted to get coffee to talk about the case, not for any other reason. Still, I felt a little brazen what with my tea and the fact that I hadn't had to pull out any stitches yet, so I wrote: *It's a date.*

When he sent back a smiling emoji, my whole body flushed.

THE NEXT MORNING, Sawyer practically dragged me to Boppy and Baba's house. He loved rock climbing, and his grandmother was an experienced climber herself. So this was their special time, and I was glad for it, both because it meant she and Sawyer got time together but also because it meant I had time to think and have a coffee with a certain handsome sheriff.

Sawyer bounced from my car seat to Lucille's, and I waved as they drove off before going in to say Hi to my dad and enjoy our Thursday morning ritual of coffee and a bacon and cheese sandwich.

My dad wasn't much of a talker, but when it was just the two of us, we went deep quickly. Years of practice made us inclined to get right to the point without pretense. The day was unseasonably warm, so we sat under the tin roof in their garden porch and ate our sandwiches at one of my dad's handmade tables.

Today, Dad didn't even make the pretense of small talk. He had a point to dive toward. "So Lucille tells me you are involved in a murder investigation over at the Scruggs place?"

Years of talking with my dad had taught me he would rarely express disapproval without asking some questions first, but the tone of this particular question let me know he was concerned, very concerned. "Not really, Dad. I found the body, but that's about it." I knew Lucille had filled him in, so the details needn't be fleshed out for him again.

When he continued to look at me, waiting for me to say more, I added, "Yesterday, the sheriff needed someone who knew a bit about old furniture when he found a skeleton key. I was the closest thing to an expert that he knew, so he asked for my help."

He nodded as he took another bite of his sandwich. "Just so long as you're not getting involved in something that doesn't concern you."

I chewed and thought about what he'd said. "I hear you, Dad, and I'm not interested in solving the murder. But there's a real story here, a story about a family who has survived and thrived a long time."

I told him what I'd learned about the Scruggs family, about Alice Scruggs in particular.

He listened and said, "You know, I knew Luther right well. He was a good man. Fair. Honest." Dad sometimes took a while to get his words going, but when he did, they were always worth hearing.

"Did you know his wife?" I asked as I savored the thick-cut bacon.

"Saw her in the store a few times. Nice enough, although I got the sense she wasn't happy with Luther."

"Yeah? How's that?"

"Just the way she looked at him," Dad said as he stacked our plates. "Like she was disappointed."

I thought of all that cash just stacked up there and wondered if that was what Mary Johnson disapproved of. Did she want to spend that money? I would have. I almost said as much, but I didn't want to interrupt Dad's story, though, so I kept quiet.

"The day he was murdered, I went up there. Wanted to pay my respects, see if there was anything they needed. I knew the church ladies would take care of the food and the kids, but I thought maybe Mary would need some help fixing things up. Maybe she'd want someone to watch the store for a few hours. Thought I could help or find someone who might." Dad sat back and stretched out his feet and said, "She slammed the door in my face."

I tilted my head. "Just like that?"

"Just like that." He stood with our plates and stared at his garden for a minute before turning to go inside. I knew that was the last I was going to hear about that from my dad, but his story made me even more determined to talk to Mary Johnson myself . . . if I could find her.

But first, I wanted to get a look at that cabinet and pick up my salvaged wares, at least the ones I could sell now. Cash was getting tight for Sawyer and me, and if I could sell any of the things I'd found, I'd have a little extra grocery money for a couple of weeks.

And I was kind of excited about coffee with the sheriff. I hugged my dad and drove on up to town. In the parking space on Main Street, I tidied my pony tail, checked to be sure the slapdash of mascara I'd applied that morning hadn't made me look like a racoon, and walked into the police station with a great deal more vim and vigor than I imagined the police station usually saw. I told the woman at the front desk who I was, and she showed me to the sheriff's office. When he answered my knock by telling me to come in, I opened the door and strolled through it like I was actually confident.

Unfortunately, my stride was stopped abruptly by the cases of soda and beer that were stacked in the middle of the small room. My wares had built a fortress in front of the sheriff's desk, and I could barely see him behind all the boxes. "Hello, Sheriff," I said from behind a stack of Cheerwine. I could feel my neck turning red from embarrassment. I really, really didn't want to be known around town as the lady who collected flat soda and skunked beer, but at this moment, that fate seemed pretty likely.

The sheriff came around the cases with what was clearly the piece of counter I'd pried up in the store in his hands. I started to take it from him, embarrassed that he was seeing the raw wares of my trade, but he didn't look puzzled at all. In fact, he looked downright enrapt. "Have you seen the details of this stuff?" he asked.

"Not really. I mean I took it because of the ads and the dates. I thought it would make a cool countertop for a funky kitchen or maybe even a tabletop. But no, I didn't look closely. Why?"

"Pokémon . . . back when it was everything to kids. My nephew collected these things by the hundreds. He and his buddies would trade them for hours." He pointed to an ad taped to the counter featuring Pikachu and packs of cards for ninety-nine cents. "I should ask him if he has any of those cards anymore."

I nodded with vigor. "You should. They might be worth a lot of money."

He sat down on a couch that I hadn't noticed what with the tower of Yuengling in the way and pointed to the seat next to him. I sat as far over on the other side of the sofa as I could, and he set the counter across our knees. "And this one for a Yahoo pager! A pager! Yahoo!" He was practically shouting with nostalgic joy.

"It's incredible, isn't it? That's part of what I love about what I do. Things that weren't that long ago can seem so foreign to us now." I pointed to a Camel ad. "Like this . . . we just don't see ads for cigarettes anymore, at least not like this." The image showed a young sailor and a woman dancing.

"Right. Now, it's just photos of the cigarette boxes themselves. It's like they've given up on trying to sell the image. They just advertise to those who already want them." The sheriff set the countertop between us, its narrow edge standing up above our knees. "I absolutely get why you do this, Paisley. It's fascinating."

I felt my palms start to sweat as he looked at me with kindness. I smiled but then looked away, too nervous to keep eye contact for long. I focused on the countertop and saw, for the first time, a bit of handwriting along the edge of the board. "What's that?"

I picked up the counter and pulled the front edge closer to my face while also trying to get the angle of the overhead light just right. "It says, 'Mary, when I'm gone, open the safe. Enough there for everything.'"

The sheriff and I looked at each other and then back at the note. "The safe," I said.

"She didn't know what he meant, did she?"

I shook my head. You'd have to know furniture to know that those kind of cabinets are called pie safes."

The sheriff ran his fingers through his black hair. "How do you have a cabinet in your house that you never open?"

I shook my head. "I have no idea. I was wondering that about Bailey Thomas, too. All that cash and neither of those women knew it was there."

Without another word, the sheriff got to his feet. "Let's look at that safe then, shall we?" He headed toward his office door, and I followed close behind.

The pie safe was in the evidence locker, which was really just a very tidy closet at the back of the sheriff's office. Once we were through the locked door, he let me take a look at the safe in the full glory of the fluorescent lights. "Can I open it?" I asked.

"Sure. We bagged all the cash, so it's just empty."

I nodded and then pulled open the right-hand door. I studied the back, and from there, I could clearly see that the door had originally been one solid piece. It looked like there had been raised panels where the punched tin now was, but the alteration was done well. Unless I had been looking for that change specifically, I wouldn't have even noticed.

I pulled the piece away from the wall and looked at the back, but there was no maker's label. "I can't tell you much, but someone definitely altered this to make it look more primitive, less impressive. And it wasn't done that long ago. These nails were put in with a nail gun."

"How can you tell?"

"They went pretty far into the wood. The person who did this used tiny nails, or they would have gone right through the other side." I ran my fingers over the front of the doors, but I couldn't feel any raised spots. "They definitely knew what they were doing."

"So they altered the cabinet in order to use it as a hiding place," the sheriff said.

"Looks like it." It was admirable work, both in craftsmanship and canny. That expression "hiding in plain sight" took on a new meaning. "Can I ask . . .?"

"$108,543."

"Are. You. Serious? There was over a hundred K in there?!"

"Yep. We couldn't believe it either, but we counted four times." The sheriff gestured toward a safe in the back of the closet. "The Jeffersons will be getting a sizeable gift once we are sure it doesn't need to remain in evidence."

I smiled. "Oh, I'm so glad they'll get the money. Did you tell them yet?"

"Nope. I didn't want to make a promise I couldn't keep, so just keep that on the downlow for now, okay?"

I let out a long breath. "Sure. Makes sense." I closed the cabinet door and stood back. "But might Mary Johnson have claim to that money? I mean it was her husband's."

The sheriff gestured to the door and then locked it behind us. "Technically no. It was abandoned in a building that belonged to the Jeffersons. We don't actually know who stowed the money there. It could have been Luther Angelis, but it might have also been his mother."

"Or his grandmother?" I felt my heart begin to race at the thought.

"Actually, that's what I wanted to talk with you about over coffee . . . if you still have time."

I stifled the mild disappointment I felt at the prospect of just talking business over our "not so much a date" date and pulled my phone out of my back pocket to check the time. "Yep, I'm still good." Sawyer and Lucille wouldn't be back for another hour.

We headed up the road to the coffee shop, and since it was still morning, I ordered a vanilla latte with whipped cream and felt a little bonus thrill when the sheriff paid for both our drinks. The thrill was tempered somewhat when he said, "Love business expenses," but I was still grateful not to spend the cash from my slim budget.

A table in the front of the shop by the window was open, so we slid into the wooden chairs and sipped our drinks quietly for a few moments. Finally, I couldn't wait to ask. "So the money? You wanted to talk with me about something?"

A small smile turned up the corners of the sheriff's mouth. "Yes, actually." His smile grew wider as he continued to sip his black coffee and look at me.

"What?" I said as a blush spread over my face.

"Nothing. It's just fun to see you excited about something." His eyes darted down to the table.

I swallowed hard and then tried to play it cool. "Patience has never been my virtue. Now tell me what's up?" I bounced up and down a little in my seat.

"Well, I think you'll be excited for a couple of reasons. First, some of the bills in the cabinet are from the early twentieth century. 1906 was the earliest."

I gasped but stayed silent because obviously the sheriff had more to say.

"And we found a note amongst the bills." He unlocked his phone and slid it toward me. "I think you'll recognize the signer."

I picked up his phone and scrolled through the letter:

My dearest daughter,

If you find this note, it will be because you have chosen to sell our store and home. Know that I support whatever choice you had to make in that regard, and I hope that what you find here serves you wherever you go whenever you need it.

With all my love,
Your Mother
3 April 1943

I LOOKED up at Sheriff Shifflett. "Do *you* know who signed the letter?" I had no idea what kind of research, if any, he'd done into the building, and I wanted to avoid embarrassing myself by oversharing if he already knew.

He shook his head. "I don't, but I'd like to. Do you know?" He put his coffee down and looked at me intently. His eyes were deep brown with flecks of gold in the irises, and I lost my train of thought for a minute when I met his gaze.

But I forced my attention back to the photo and said, "Given the date, I think this note is from Alice Scruggs to her daughter

Sheila, Luther Angelis's mother." I told Sheriff Shifflett the quick genealogy on the family and told him about how Alice had inherited the store from her father. "They must have been saving money in that cabinet for almost a hundred years."

The sheriff nodded and put his phone back in his pocket when I slid it back across the table. "Well, that definitely means the money belongs to the Jeffersons. I had a clear case given the state of the building, but this letter cinches it. Thanks."

"Sheriff Shifflett, I've been researching an article about the Scruggs Store for my newsletter. I won't mention the money, of course, but it won't disrupt things for me to publish the article, will it?" I found myself holding my breath waiting for his answer.

"First, call me Santiago." He smiled at me, and I noticed the way his eye tooth on the right-side of his mouth was just a little out of alignment with the rest. "Secondly, what you are writing is public knowledge. As long as you don't reveal anything about our active case, you don't need to worry."

I smiled. "Thank you, *Santiago*. That's a relief. I don't want to get in your way at all." I leaned back. "I am hoping to talk to Mary Johnson, though, to see what she knew about Luther's family. Is that a problem?"

"Nope. But if you find out anything in your research that you think I should know—"

I didn't let him finish. "I have your number."

"Use it, Paisley . . . and if you get into trouble, you do have a tail, remember?" He put out his hand to shake mine. "Thank you, Paisley. You have been really helpful."

I shook his hand, and he held it just a bit longer than necessary. I gave his fingers a little squeeze and then quickly picked up my half-finished drink to take with me.

With a wave, he headed back to the station, and I walked to Mika's store. I had a few minutes, and I needed to tell her about that conversation, or at least part of it.

Fortunately, my best friend's shop was full of people who seemed quite self-sufficient, so when I tugged her to the back corner and told her about the "Call me Santiago" and the lingering handshake, her squeal didn't catch their attention.

"Oh, Paisley. What are you thinking about that?" Her shoulders were up by her ears, and her grin showed all her teeth. "He is very handsome."

I blushed. "I don't know what I'm thinking, honestly, but it is flattering." I started to head back to the front of the store, but as I went, I said over my shoulder, "He *is* handsome."

I could hear Mika's giggle all the way out the door. The two of us were squarely in our forties, but something about dating made us act like teenagers again. It was kind of fun.

Just as I was climbing into my car, my phone rang, and Lucille's voice was matched only in enthusiasm by Sawyer's squeals in the background. "Your son wants to ask you something," she spat out before Sawyer commandeered the phone.

"Mama, Baba take me to see horses, okay?"

Lucille came back on the line. "There's a petting zoo at Maymont, and I was wondering if Saw and I could make our morning date into a full-day date." She took a second to calm Sawyer down before she spoke into the phone again. "Sorry, I probably should have asked you before I told him about the animals."

I laughed. "I think a Saw–Baba Day sounds perfect. He will need some lunch, though."

"Right. You don't mind chicken nuggets and French fries?" she asked.

"Only if you also get him a milkshake," I said just as Saw shouted, "And a milkshake."

"A brown one?" Lucille asked him.

"Yep," he said.

"Just remember to say the word *chocolate* at the drive-through. Trust me when I say they get confused when you order the brown one." I heard her laugh, and then my son's cackles grew loud again. "Have fun. I'll have my phone if you need me."

"See you about four," she added and was off.

I loved hearing him have so much fun with his grand-mother. And while I would miss my boy, I also loved that I now had a full afternoon to do research. I checked my email, saw I had nothing pressing, and headed back to the coffee shop with my emergency twenty from the envelope in my dashboard. I usually kept the cash there for a real emergency – low on gas, toddler meltdown that required a cookie, or some such – but today, it was going to pay for me to have a chicken Caesar wrap and a vanilla steamer. A full day to work was a luxury to be treasured.

I ordered my food and drink and took the same table the sheriff, *Santiago*, and I had shared and pulled out my laptop. Within minutes, I had located Mary Johnson's address, right near where I sat in downtown Octonia. It was amazing what the internet could draw up. Just to be sure though, I checked the GIS map, and sure enough, the property address was owned by a Mary Johnson. Now, I just had to come up with a reason to stop by.

I could go with the truth, but given what my father and Berlinda had told me about her, I didn't think Ms. Johnson would take kindly to me prying into her marriage to Luther Angelis. I needed a different angle, so I studied the GIS map near her house. Fortunately, I saw a historic black church just up the street and decided that I could say I was researching the church building. It had been there since just after Emancipation, and I knew a few of the members. They had, in fact, been asking me to come see the old pastor's house on the property. It was slated to be torn down, and they thought I might be able to help them determine what was of value to save. I had kept putting it off, but maybe now I could use their

request for this story AND get a head start on a future newsletter article.

I was feeling good about my plan when my wrap arrived, so
I took the next few minutes to eat and do a little further digging
into Berlinda's family tree online. Given that Berlinda's mother,
Sheila, hadn't listed her father on her marriage license, I didn't
think it likely I'd find it anywhere else, but I did a little
searching anyway. I looked for Sheila's death certificate,
knowing that they often contained the names of their parents,
but the space for Father's Name simply said "Unknown." I
scanned all the vital records I could find online about Sheila
and then about Alice, but nothing showed the name of the man
who was Berlinda's grandfather. I was going to have to resort to
the best resource for information in the rural South – gossip.

But that search would have to wait. My delicious wrap was
history, and I needed to go dig up some of the other kind of
history over at Mary Johnson's house. I was glad I had worn my
tennis shoes because this was going to be a feet-on-the-ground
kind of afternoon.

I couldn't just stroll up to Mary Johnson's house and then
head home. Nope, I had to build my cover story, and if I really
was going to turn this into an actual story, then I needed to talk
to as many people as I could. I grabbed one of the endless
supply of reusable totes out of the back of my car, dropped in
my notebook and a pen, and began the walk to Bethel Baptist. I
figured I would start by the church and knock on doors up the
street and then back down the other side. Johnson's house was
right in the middle, so that many visits should not only disguise
my primary motivation but also give me a lot of information
about the church's history.

At the first house I visited, an ancient woman with skin as
smooth as glass invited me in for tea and then had me filling
pages and pages of notes about who was buried in the church
cemetery next door, who the pastors had been and, more inter-

estingly, why they'd left, and also about the quite impressive list of charitable works the church members did. She was a treasure, but by the time she and I were done, I'd been there over an hour. I couldn't spend time like that with everyone, so I made a new plan.

Next door, I knocked, told the man who answered that I was gathering names of people who might like to be interviewed about the church, and took down his information when he said he'd be happy to help. Three more doors brought me two more volunteers and a promise from a teenage girl to give her grandmother my number. These people were profoundly helpful, and I found myself looking forward to my new story in its own right.

That feeling died back a bit when I realized Mary Johnson's house was up next. Given what Berlinda and Dad had said, I wasn't hopeful that my visit would be welcome, but I had to try. I knocked, took a step back, and half-wished no one would answer. But sure enough, a black woman with graying hair and a "My Blood Type Is Pumpkin Spice" sweatshirt came to the door and smiled. "Can I help you?"

"Hi. My name is Paisley Sutton. I'm a historian, and I'm doing research on Bethel Church. Do you have a few minutes to talk?"

"Oh, sure, come in," the woman said pleasantly.

I followed her into a tidy cottage with a very modern look – all grays and whites with highlights of shimmering pink. It wasn't my style, but it was lovely and well-done. "Your house is beautiful. Thanks for talking with me."

She smiled and pointed to the couch. "I don't know how much help I can be. I only moved here twenty years ago, and in this neighborhood, that makes me a newcomer."

I laughed because the woman I'd spoken with earlier had said basically that about most of her neighbors, even though I imagined some of them had lived there all their lives. "I get it. If you and your parents weren't born in Octonia, you'll never be from here."

"Ah, so you are from here then?" she said with a laugh.

"Yep, and my parents, too." I took out my notebook and pen and looked at her. "Do you mind if I take a few notes?"

"Oh, no, not at all. What are you writing about the church?"

I told her about the women I knew who had been asking me to come salvage in the pastor's house and that I thought it would be good to know about the place and the people before I went digging around. "I'll be happy to send you a copy of the article when it's ready if you'd like."

"I'd love that. Thanks," she said as she leaned back in her ecru chair and a half.

She was beginning to relax, and I knew that this was the time for me to ask the questions. "Do you mind sharing your name and email so I can send it over when it's ready in a few weeks?"

"I'm Mary Johnson." She smiled and gave me her email.

At least I was talking to the right woman. "And you said you moved here about twenty years ago?"

"That's right. Just after my husband died." She spoke more quietly.

"I see. I'm sorry for your loss. If you don't mind me asking, where did you live before this? In Octonia County?"

"Oh yes, down the road a bit. My husband owned a convenience store just south of town."

I swallowed and said as innocently as I could. "Not, by chance, Scruggs Store."

She furrowed her brow. "Actually yes. You know it?"

"I do. I'm writing about it, too." I explained that I had just done a salvage job there and that I had become interested in the store's history because of that. "I realize that may feel invasive since maybe you lived there, too?"

She waved a hand. "Actually, I like the idea of something of that old place being saved. It wasn't the happiest time in my life living there. I had a little boy then, and Luther had to be in the store all the time. It was just hard, but the building was beautiful."

"I'm the single mom of a two-year-old, so I hear you. It's hard having to be the one to do all the things." I was surprised at how much I liked Mary, at how much I related to her. "I guess you heard what happened at the store earlier this week?"

Mary sighed. "I did. Poor woman. The story I heard was that she was living there. Do you know if that's true?" Mary's tone had gotten suddenly much brighter, much more invested than thirty seconds ago.

I shrugged. On principle, I did my best not to lie, but I wasn't about to reveal what I knew because I'd promised Santiago but also because in this case GI Joe was right: knowledge is power. "I'm not sure. Did you ever know much of the history of the place, like who built it?"

She didn't answer my question but asked one of her own. "They'll be looking around out there, I guess? The police I mean."

I nodded. "I guess so. Anything they need to know?"

"No, no nothing," she said too quickly and with a tone that told me this line of conversation was closed, although she still looked like a woman whose curiosity, or something, had been piqued.

"So you don't know much about the history of the building or anything like that?" I asked again.

Mary shrugged and shifted back in her seat before looking out her front window. "It was some relative of Luther's, his grandmother or something. I never paid much attention to that stuff."

I felt my historian's defensiveness starting to rise and talked myself back down. "Luther ever tell you anything about the building itself. Any little tidbit might make a great part of the article?" I was really fishing now, but I had to keep trying because she might know the key to discovering Luther's grandfather's name.

She tilted her head and then met my eyes again. "Actually, now that you mention it, he did say that they built the store and the house from trees they felled on that land itself. He was always telling my son a story about how they had to cut the trees down and then let them cure for months before they could saw them into logs and planks to build." She raised her shoulders to her ears. "Don't know if that's of interest or not."

I smiled. "It definitely is. It means that building is not just built on the land where it sits, but from it, too. That's a great bit of history. Thanks."

Mary stretched and looked quickly at the clock on the wall beside her. She was ready for me to go.

"Do you have time for one more question?" I knew I was pressing my luck here, but I had to ask. "Did Luther ever mention his grandfather, his mother's father?"

Her eyes cut to mine. "Why do you ask?" There was definite wariness in her voice.

"Oh, just curiosity, honestly. I was looking into the history of the store, and I saw that his grandmother didn't list a husband. But of course, we know she had a child, Luther's mom. At the time, it might have been quite hard for her to have a child without being married. She also ran that store all by herself. I'm so impressed by her, so I just wanted to learn more about her life and the people around her." That was the total truth, but I did make sure I didn't mention the Jeffersons just in case she felt about them the way Berlinda did about her.

"I don't know much. Luther looked into it for a bit because his mother wouldn't talk about her parents. But if he ever figured out who the man was, he never told me." She looked at me and smiled. "You are a curious person, huh? You like looking into things like this?"

I nodded. "I do. It's why I went into history. I love hunting down the answers to questions." I smiled as I stood up from my chair. "Thanks for answering mine, and I will send the article on the church when I write it. Thanks. I'd best be off to see your neighbors now." I was realizing as I headed toward the door that I hadn't asked much about the church, but clearly, she was ready for our conversation to be over. I didn't even try to shore up my cover.

"I'll look forward to it . . . and if I think of anything about Alice or Henry, I'll let you know. Thanks for coming by." She held the door and watched me as I went down the front steps and over to her neighbor's house.

Alice or Henry, I thought. I hadn't mentioned Luther's grandmother's name, but Mary had known it. And who exactly was Henry?

7

I did visit a couple more houses on Mary's street, but I was too eager to look up the name Henry in the public records to do more than gather a few more names for later contact. I scribbled contact information in my notebook and then hoofed it back to my car, where I could just get enough Wi-Fi from the church to load the genealogy site.

A quick search of the name Henry with a birthdate around the time I expected and in Octonia yielded too many results to be useful. I tried adding in the search term "Alice" and got no results. So that meant a man named Henry who was approximately her age wasn't affiliated with her in any official document that the site kept, and thus, it was unlikely they were legally connected at all.

That easy and quick resource exhausted, I turned to a newspaper search. Soon, I was scouring every article in the local Octonia paper that mentioned a Henry in the decade before and the decade after Sheila's birth. Finally, in a tiny piece buried in the middle of the paper from 1922, I saw something that captured my attention.

Henry Lewis, age 32, elected as sheriff of Octonia County. Sheriff

*Lewis is a lifelong resident of Octonia and was elected by the popu-
lace to serve a two-year term as sheriff for the county. When asked
for comment, he said, "I look forward to helping make Octonia a safer
place for my children, Stan, Susan, and Sheila, and everyone in
Octonia.*

HENRY LEWIS, Sheriff Henry Lewis, had a daughter named
Sheila. His name was pretty common, which meant genealogy
work was harder – a tiny part of me chose Sawyer's name
because it was unusual, and I knew genealogists and historians
in the future would thank me – but I couldn't imagine there'd
be that many Henry Lewises in Octonia in the early twentieth
century. When I factored in that anyone elected sheriff at that
time was almost certainly white, I found him in the 1930 census
in seconds.

I fleshed out his family tree – wife, children, grandchildren,
and even great-grandchildren – but there was no official record
of a daughter named Sheila, and I didn't find any other
researcher's family trees listing her either.

A quick review of Sheriff Lewis's life story revealed that he
was a World War I veteran and worked for the police department when he returned. He was elected to the sheriff's office at
age thirty-two, served for four terms, and then became a county
supervisor before retiring at sixty-five. He died in 1962 at the age
of seventy-two. A good life by all accounts.

And yet, there was this secret, that wasn't really, given that
he'd named Sheila in his quote for the paper. He claimed her, it
seemed, but she wasn't listed on any legal document as his
child.

I felt certain that Sheila Scruggs was his daughter, but I had
no proof. And while I was fairly sure I could find his grandchildren, or maybe even his children, by just asking around, I
figured I better have pretty solid footing before I talked to

someone's descendants about their long-lost aunt, especially since that aunt was a black woman.

A quick glance at my phone told me I still had at least an hour before Lucille was home with Sawyer, so I went to the best source of local stories I knew and drove back to see my dad.

He was in the backyard staining chopping blocks he'd made out of recycled wood and singing loudly to some oldies station. My dad loved a good tune, and I loved to hear him sing. I was almost sorry to interrupt. Almost.

"Daddy?" I said as I caught his attention so he wouldn't be startled if I got too close without him hearing me. "Got a minute?"

"Uh-oh, she pulled out *Daddy*, so I know she needs something." He grinned at me and turned off the CD player. "What do you need?"

"Did you know Sheriff Lewis when you were a kid?" I asked as I sat down on a low stone wall near his workshop.

Dad took out his handkerchief and wiped sawdust from his face. "Well, there's a blast from the past. I haven't thought about that man in a long time." He eased himself down onto the wall next to me. "I did know him. He coached my little league team. As I remember it, he had a pretty mean slider."

I hoped I would remember to ask my dad for pictures of himself in his baseball uniform at another time, but right now, I had a task to accomplish and limited toddler-free time to do it. "A good guy then?"

Dad squinted at me but then said, "One of the best, actually. I was too little to understand it, but he gave a lot of help to a lot of people, and not in the way you might expect a sheriff to help."

I leaned back and tried to look casual, even while I was fully aware that my dad could read my body language better than anyone living. "What do you mean?"

"You're onto something, huh? Something about Sheriff

Lewis?" Dad leaned toward me with a twinkle in his eye. "You want to tell me now or later?"

"Later," I said as I gave up the pretense of relaxation and turned fully toward him. "I want to hear what you have to say without you knowing what I have to tell you."

He nodded. "Well, the law wasn't always fair for everybody back in my day. But the sheriff was, if you know what I mean."

Now, he really had my attention. "Do you mean he didn't enforce unjust laws?"

Dad laughed. "Well, I don't know that he would have gone as far as to say all that, but he held the same standard of the law for everybody, no matter what they looked like." My father took my hand. "He was good like that."

I smiled and squeezed Dad's fingers. "So he wasn't a bigot?"

"Nope. Not at all. He spent a lot of time with all the people he was elected to serve and protect, knew their stories, too. There was this little black boy on my team, Hennie Hempstead. Some of the white parents said they wouldn't let their boys play on the sheriff's team if Hennie did. Said some awful hateful things about Hennie and to him, too." Dad put his other hand over mine. "Sheriff Lewis put a stop to the ugliness toward Hennie, but then he let those parents speak their piece. When they'd finished shouting, he said, 'I hear there are some other mighty fine teams in this league. I'm sure your boys will do just fine on any of them.'"

"He didn't argue? Didn't try to show them how wrong they were?" I blurted.

"No use, Baby Girl. You can't argue with stupid." Dad winked at me. "But he coached Hennie through that whole season, and we had a good team. We went undefeated."

I smiled at my dad and his memories, and I felt all the tension of the day fade away. "You have a point, Daddy."

"Now, tell me what you've got." He pulled me to my feet and then led me over to the rocking chairs beneath his back porch.

I decided to begin with the hook, just like I would in my story. "Sheriff Lewis had a black daughter. Sheila Scruggs."

Dad whistled through his teeth. "Well, that is something. But that makes sense. Black folks were always at our games, and when he ran for board of supervisors, the black vote was what got him his seat. I remember Mama and Daddy talking about it."

"Were they happy he won?" I didn't know if I wanted to hear his answer, but I had to ask.

"I think so. They didn't talk much with me about politics, you know, but I think so." He smiled.

I let out a sigh of relief and then told Dad the rest of what I'd learned about the Scruggs family. I was on such a tear of storytelling that I almost blurted out that we'd found over a hundred thousand dollars in the building, but I stopped myself just in time.

"Girl, you know how to research. Way to go. Now, what's next?" He rocked a bit in his chair as he put his usual toothpick in his mouth. My dad was country boy all the way, and I loved it.

"Well, first, after you, of course, I need to tell the Jeffersons. And then the sheriff. This may be tied up with the murders in the store."

Dad stopped rocking and sat up in his chair. "You remember what I said this morning, Baby Girl?"

"I do, Daddy, and that's why I'm telling the sheriff. I don't need to have any part in figuring out the murders. I'm just interested in the history."

"The mystery of history," he said with a smile. "You should use that, just give me credit, okay?"

I smiled and then paused when I realized I hadn't yet named my newsletter. "I think I will. The Mystery of History newsletter has a nice ring to it."

At that moment, I heard a small voice bellow "Mama" from

the side yard, and a few seconds later, a toddler head rammed into my chest.

"Hi, Saw. It's good to see you. Did you have fun with Baba?" I snuggled my boy into my lap.

"Uh-huh," he said as he wrapped his arms around my neck and hugged me. "I petted a donkey."

"You did?"

The rest of the conversation was a detailed account of all the animals Sawyer had petted and how high he had climbed, and by the time he was done, I was worn out just from the listening.

Lucille seized the opportunity to invite us to stay for dinner when Saw headed toward the garden to "dig for worms." "I'm making yellow cake with chocolate icing," she said as she waggled her eyebrows.

"For dinner? If so, I'm in!" I said with a quick look at my phone. Only four. "We'd love to stay, but we'll need to leave by six. Does that suit your schedule?"

"Are you kidding? Your dad already has chili in the crock-pot, and I can make cornbread in ten minutes." She headed toward the door. "Just let me get things baking, and we can eat in thirty and have dessert in less than an hour."

"Perfect," I said, but then remembered. "Dad, is it beef in the chile or venison? Tell me the truth."

"Beef," he said with a wry smile, "but I bet you couldn't tell the difference if I was lying."

I rolled my eyes over to Lucille and waited for her to speak. "Definitely beef. I saw the package."

"Thank you," I said. "We'd love to stay. Can I help?"

"No, I help," Sawyer said as he ran back over covered in dirt but thankfully wormless.

"Okay, Sawyer, but first, we wash your hands," Lucille said as she scooped him up.

"I'm glad you married her, Dad. At least she tells me the

truth." I slapped him on the leg and went inside to help wrangle the sous chef.

AT HOME THAT NIGHT, somehow Sawyer talked me into taking a bath with him, so there I was in my bathing suit in my own bathtub being splashed by a toddler. It wasn't the relaxing image of a bath that I often relished, but it was really fun . . . and it spent the last of the little guy's energy, so when I laid him in bed, he was asleep before he could even say "again" when I finished the story of Little Red Riding Hood.

The day had been exhausting for me, too. My mind was all keyed up, and I needed a long, slow wind-down. I was grateful to have stitches and TV to watch. I was working my way across the canopy of the carousel using the technique my mom had taught me. I picked a color and then worked through the whole thread, stitching everything within easy distance that used that shade. As I went, I marked the squares on the pattern off in pencil.

I knew some cross-stitchers worked a block of ten squares by ten squares at a time, but I found that difficult for me, mostly because I hated even wasting those extra bits of thread I had to sacrifice to begin and end a section. I preferred to follow something through to its natural conclusion, which is maybe why I liked historical and genealogical research so much. It was a story that ended, so to speak, in today. The story itself would go on, of course, but I couldn't know where it would go. I could just find what existed for now and let the story, on paper at least, end there.

Tonight, while I sewed and pondered my day, I turned on *Midsomer Murders*. I felt like watching something quaint and charming, and I needed a little mystery to keep my attention while my brain processed what I'd learned that day. I meant what I'd said to Dad about not getting involved in the murder investigation, too, but I couldn't help feeling like there was something I hadn't quite put together yet from my day's research, and I wondered if Chief Inspector Barnaby might not just inspire me to tie up the loose ends.

Unfortunately, fatigue caught up with me before I made much headway on the sewing or the murder solving, and I woke up two hours and two dead bodies later with a stiff neck and a cat playing with my embroidery floss. I packed up the sewing, scooped up the cat, and climbed into bed. All mysteries could wait until morning.

BEFORE FIRST LIGHT the next day, Sawyer and I spent a good hour running his wooden vehicles around his toy village. The police car made a lot of trips between the barn and the hospital. But then my son was very committed to watching "dogs and kitties" on YouTube, and I took the opportunity to step into my "office," aka the back-bedroom closet, and make my phone calls.

First, I wanted to tell Berlinda. It was her family, her story, so she deserved the first call. Plus, I couldn't wait to hear what she thought of this news. I realized it might not be a story she wanted told widely, given how prominent her grandfather had been in the community, but I knew she'd want to know. And if she didn't want me to share the information further than the sheriff, who I felt obligated to tell, I wouldn't.

Berlinda answered her cell with a cheerful, "Good Morning, Paisley. To what do I owe this pleasure?"

I smiled and sat down on the floor of the closet with Sawyer's pants grazing the top of my head. "Well, I found something, and I thought you'd like to know about it. Do you have a moment?"

"I'm retired. I have lots of moments. Just let me get George. I told him all you shared with me on Wednesday, and he is mightily invested now, too." She pulled the phone away from her ear and called for her husband.

I took the opportunity to quietly peek out and be sure Sawyer wasn't elbow deep in the bag of sugar, a lesson I'd learned from experience. But fortunately, the dogs and cats must have been particularly funny today because he and Beauregard were still quite engrossed in the screen as they cuddled on the couch.

"Okay," Berlinda said, her voice a bit echo-ey since I was now on speaker, "we're ready."

"Hi George," I began by explaining that I'd talked to some people in town and gotten some leads. I decided to forego giving away my sources, just in case Berlinda didn't like this news and had more reason to dislike Mary Johnson. I had enjoyed my conversation with the woman and didn't want to taint my news with the mention of her name. I said, "One woman mentioned Alice and Henry in passing when I was leaving. I hadn't told her your grandmother's name, but since she knew it and paired it with Henry, I thought that might be something to go on."

Berlinda cleared her throat. "Pardon my interruption, Paisley, but how do you think she knew the name Henry?"

George said, "Berlinda, we don't even know why the name Henry matters. Let the woman finish her story." The tone of his voice was gentle, but it was urgent, too. He *really* wanted to hear the story.

"Let's come back to that because I have a theory to explain what she knew and how. But first, let me tell you what I figured out, okay?" I was near bursting with the news, but I also wanted to suss out my theory with Berlinda when we could focus on it.

"Totally fine, Paisley. Please continue," Berlinda said.

I sighed. "Your grandfather is, as best I can tell, Berlinda, Henry Lewis." I stopped there, giving them a chance to take in the name and react without me filling in any gaps.

The silence was extended, but I knew that big news could take a minute to sink in. I took the moment to check on Sawyer, and he was now in the bathroom next to me washing his Baby. Poor Baby, it looked like she might be drowning. But Saw was content, so I pulled the door shut quietly again.

I could hear a little movement on the other side of the phone, but neither Berlinda or George had said anything yet. "Should I take this silence to mean you know who that is?"

George's voice was loud in the phone. "Berlinda is a little overwhelmed, Paisley."

"Oh no," I said. "I'm so sorry. I was hoping this would be neutral news at worst."

"No, don't misunderstand me. She's overwhelmed with joy." He took the phone away from his mouth and said, "Right, dear? It's joy that's making you cry."

When he spoke into the phone again, he said, "Definitely joy. Perhaps I should explain."

"Please." I prayed Baby could withstand a full scrub-down because I wanted to hear this.

"When Berlinda was in high school, Supervisor Lewis took note of her academic prowess and offered her a scholarship to attend the Virginia college of her choice." George's voice took on the deepening tenor of a natural storyteller, and I found myself imagining the two of them as fresh-faced teenagers, him in dress pants and a button down, her in a poodle skirt and bobby socks. "Berlinda talked to her mother and father, and with a few more conversations with Supervisor Lewis, they accepted what they thought would be a few hundred dollars to offset the cost of Berlinda's attendance at Virginia State."

The Historically Black University was a stellar institution, had been since it was founded, and, given the time period, I could only imagine what an opportunity this was for Berlinda. "Wow, what a generous offer."

"Actually, it gets better," George said with a smile in his

voice. "When Berlinda arrived, she discovered that her tuition for all four years had been paid in full. The donor was anonymous, but she knows that Supervisor Lewis paid for her schooling."

A small head peeked into the closet, and I gestured to Sawyer to sit down. He plopped into my lap and nestled his head against my chest. At rare moments, he knew the importance of a quiet conversation.

"That's incredible. And he never said a word?" I asked.

The phone rustled in my ear, and Berlinda came on the line. "No, not one word. But we never got the scholarship check he promised either, so I think it's safe to say he was my benefactor. Now, I know why." I could hear the tears in her voice. "Thank you, Paisley."

"Oh, you're most welcome, Berlinda." I circled back to "my sources" slip up about Alice and Henry. I knew my time was running short because a certain little boy was getting fidgety. "So here's what I'm thinking. I think this person heard something or found something that told them about Henry Lewis."

"You think so?" Berlinda's voice was excited. "But how would they know? You think this person is hiding something?"

"I don't know. Maybe?" I didn't get the impression that Mary was being cagey, but she definitely wasn't telling me everything she knew. I just didn't know why. "But it might be worth asking. If it's okay with you, I can do it, but I wanted to ask your permission before I went back."

"Oh, please do ask, Paisley. I'd like to know how this person knew about my grandfather." Berlinda got choked up again.

I couldn't blame her. And if she had known my source was Mary Johnson, her former sister-in-law, I knew she'd want to know even more. If my brother knew something about my family that I didn't know, I wasn't sure how I'd feel. Given, though, that my brother had about as much interest in family lore as Sawyer did in eating brussels sprouts, I didn't have much need to be concerned.

"I'll ask, Berlinda, and I'll let you know what I learn as soon as I do."

Just then, a tiny hand went up and grabbed my phone. "No talk, Mama," Sawyer said as he ran out the door with the phone.

I just had enough time to shout, "Sorry, Berlinda and George. Talk soon," before Sawyer tapped the screen and hung up with the sounds of their laughter in the background.

For the next ten minutes, I tried to act like I wasn't chasing my son around the house to get my phone when I was, in fact, chasing my son. Finally, though, he tired of my nonchalance and tossed the phone on the couch before beginning a heart-stopping routine of somersaulting off the back of said couch. Never a dull moment.

Clearly, I was not going to be able to call the sheriff with my news about Henry Lewis, so I decided it was time to introduce Sawyer to the world of law enforcement. "Saw, want to go see police officers?"

"Right now. I ready," he said and went to stand by the door.

I texted the sheriff, told him I was coming by with some news, and asked if Sawyer could see his patrol car. I could see the unmarked car sitting at the edge of our driveway, and I knew they had lights and sirens in there. But I didn't want Sawyer to get overly interested in our security both for the sake of the officers who might not relish *constant* company from a toddler and for the sake of a toddler who might just get a little scared if he put it together that we needed a security detail.

The sheriff responded immediately. *Meet me in the parking lot. We'll do a ride along. I'll put the car seat in.*

To know a man who would take my son on a ride in his police car and who had a car seat ready for such a ride made my heart flutter. I took a long sip of the glass of water I'd poured myself two hours ago and tried to calm down.

Then, I scooped up Sawyer's backpack, slid his arms into a coat, and dropped a few treats for Beauregard, who eyed them nonchalantly and then went back to sleep.

It's amazing what the promise of a ride in a police car can do for a two-year-old. He was in his seat and buckling it before I even wedged myself beside him to do the straps. I was going to have to think of incentives like this more often. Lollipops held nothing compared to sirens and lights apparently.

As I drove the few miles into town, I tried to take deep breaths and keep my mind focused on the former sheriff instead of the current one. I was mostly successful until, that is, I saw Santiago leaning against his cruiser. Then, I lost all thoughts on all trains, not just that one.

Fortunately, my son is charming and cute, and his shyness and excitement smoothed over my tongue-tied greeting when we arrived. Soon, we had him strapped into a car seat in the back, and I was cracking jokes about how I might just need this cage between him and me in our Subaru. "You have no idea how hard it is to focus when a juice cup hits you in the back of the head."

Santiago looked at me out of the corner of his eye and then adjusted the rearview mirror. "Sawyer Sutton, do you throw things at your mom when she's driving? Am I understanding this correctly?" He'd adopted the serious voice of a TV police officer.

I turned around to see Sawyer's eyes wide and his head nodding. "Sorry, Policeman," he said.

"Well, thank you for apologizing, young man, but you must also give me your word you will not throw anything at your mom again. That is very dangerous." I could see a hint of a smile coming onto Santiago's face.

"I won't," Saw said very seriously.

"Good," Santiago said. "Now, do you want to hear the siren?"

A grin broke out over my son's face, and I knew the one on mine was just as big. "It might be loud, Sawyer."

"It won't be loud, Mama," he said with all seriousness.

"Okay, here goes." The siren sounded out across the fields outside of town, and Sawyer laughed and laughed.

After a few miles, Sawyer grew bored with the siren, and Santiago passed his radio through the screen between us. "You sure that's a good idea?" I asked.

"I set the channel to one we don't use and asked the dispatcher to talk with Saw if he figured out the buttons. They'll both enjoy it." He took his eyes off the road for one second to smile at me. "Besides, it'll give you a chance to tell me what you learned."

I had almost forgotten about the actual purpose of this visit, what with the pheromones coursing through me and the sheriff's sweetness and all, but I was still eager to tell him about it.

After I gave him the run-down on Mary Johnson and Berlinda and George's story, he said, "Well, that is an interesting twist to this, especially considering what we figured out this morning."

"Oh?" I didn't want to appear too eager to be involved in police business, given my dad's warning and my own genuine desire to stay out of it, but I couldn't stop my curiosity.

"Well, this morning, one of the guys who was set to demo the place went back to study the building for the best strategy for that work. He had our permission to be there, as long as he didn't go into the back bedroom." He cleared his throat, and I saw a little color travel up his neck. "Well, he had to, um, take a leak, so he stepped into the woods behind the house. He wanted to be sure he was well away from the road and walked pretty far in."

I leaned toward him in my seat. "And?"

"And he found a massive, old crop of marijuana. The biologist we called said plants can self-seed and come back year after year if they get some care. We think that's what's been happening given the old, dead plants we found amongst the living ones." Santiago shot a glance at me.

"I know absolutely nothing about marijuana, but could it have been hemp?" I felt naïve asking, but I believe in thinking the best in every situation until I couldn't do that anymore.

"Nope, this was the good stuff, the smoking stuff. The biologist from Virginia Tech is coming in later this afternoon to take a look. Thinks he can tell us about how long ago the patch was planted."

I sighed and thought back over my conversation with Mary Johnson. It had seemed like she was not telling me something. "Maybe Luther Angelis planted it?"

Santiago nodded. "That's what I'm wondering. If so, it might explain a few things."

"Like why he had over a hundred K hidden in that cabinet?" I said.

"And why someone might have killed him."

I suddenly realized Sawyer had gone very quiet, and when I turned around to look, I saw he was fast asleep, Santiago's radio hugged to his chest. "Oh no," I said quietly, even as I admired his perfect, sleeping face.

Santiago looked into the rearview mirror and said, "No problem. Fancy a drive up on the parkway?"

The part of the Blue Ridge Parkway known as Skyline Drive was just up the mountain at the edge of Octonia County. I didn't get up there nearly as much as I'd like partially because of the cost of the park pass but also because I had visions of losing my son over the edge of a scenic overlook.

But today, I couldn't resist the chance to just ride and take in the view, especially with such good company. "You can be away that long?"

"I took the security shift for you this afternoon. So technically, I'm on duty." He winked and then gestured to the console. "I always pack some Nabs and sodas in case I miss a meal. Help yourself."

I opened up the arm rest between us and took out two packs of cheddar and peanut butter crackers and two of those tiny Pepsis that were great for calorie counting but never quite enough. "Open them for you?" I asked.

Santiago nodded and then gratefully accepted a cracker. "Now, tell me what theories you have about how all this ties together," he said.

I munched on my own cracker as I thought about that. "Can I ask a question first?"

"Yep," he said as he took another cracker from his pack.

"Did you figure out what that red-headed man was doing at the store the other day?" I had some sense that he fit into this somehow, but I wasn't sure how.

"Oh yeah, we did. His name is Victor Davison. He's a local guy. Handyman type. Does odd jobs for folks, taking down trees, digging ditches, that kind of thing."

"Did he say why he was at the store?" I knew I was getting too far into things with my questions, but somehow, I felt like maybe I'd been on that path to "involved" ever since I asked for the salvage job.

"He did. Said he just wanted to be sure the building was secure. But I expect he was lying." The sheriff gave his head a little shake.

"You're sure?"

"I'm sure. No one just stops by an abandoned building that they've driven past hundreds of times out of curiosity." He gave me a side-eyed glance. "Okay, maybe you do. But most people don't."

I grinned. "I totally do, but I see what you mean. So you think Davison has something to do with the pot?"

Santiago nodded and took another cracker from the packet in my hand. "I think he may have a lot to do with it. It's clear someone's been harvesting back there recently. Steadily, too. Not wholesale like they do in a lot of operations, where they plant, grow, and then clear out. Here it's more like selective harvesting."

"So the stand stays intact," I said as I watched the gorgeous valleys and hollows of Virginia pass below us. Sawyer was still snoozing hard.

"Right. You know something about growing pot that you aren't telling me?" The sheriff smiled out of the corner of his mouth.

"Nope. Not a thing about pot. But I've lived around here my whole life and watched people timber their land. Some clear-cut, some selectively harvest. I understand why people do both, but it's amazing how whole the forest looks when it's selectively harvested." I didn't bother to add that I also thought clear-cutting made the land look barren, apocalyptic.

Santiago laughed. "Well, it's the same with marijuana. It grows stronger and more potent if it's allowed to naturally reproduce."

"So very much like a forest then?"

"Yep. But don't go spreading that information around. Growing marijuana isn't legal in Virginia."

"Not yet." I laughed.

He shook his head and then seemed to drift off into his own thoughts. I smiled and leaned my head back and studied the mountains. Most of the color had fallen from the trees already, but I loved this time of year when the golden trees – the beeches mostly – held their leaves the longest. On a day like today, when the sun was bright, the mountains looked decorated with lights.

I closed my eyes and let my mind play with this new information. Someone had been tending this stand for a very long time, and clearly, given what Santiago said, it was of value to the person or people who were taking care of it. I wondered if Bailey Thomas had come across it. Maybe she'd seen someone harvesting and been a threat. Or maybe someone had seen her and wanted to be sure she didn't become a threat.

I pushed that line of thought out of my mind though. That was Santiago's job, not mine. What I was curious about was if this marijuana operation could have been related to Luther Angelis's murder. If so, how? And was that where all the money came from?

It felt likely that the money was tied to this somehow. It just didn't seem likely that someone who ran a convenience store on a rural road in the middle of the mountains made enough money to put away over a hundred thousand dollars, even over decades. But then, that money had been accumulating since the 1920s. Maybe if I skipped out on bi-weekly maple bacon bagel from Murphy's I might be able to save up that much cash over time, but I doubted it. I was pretty frugal, and I couldn't even manage to save a hundred dollars a month. But then, Murphy's Bagels wasn't around when Luther, Sheila, or Alice were alive, so maybe I was being too hard on myself.

I was smiling and thinking about how much I loved that cinnamon pistachio cream cheese when a voice disrupted what was apparently my dream. "Mama, wake up!"

I sat forward with a start of embarrassment and looked over my shoulder to see Sawyer grinning in this newly devilish way he had when he realized he'd caught me doing something he thought I shouldn't do, like sleep. Then, I looked at the man behind the wheel of the car, and he was grinning, too. These two could be trouble.

When I stretched, I caught a glimpse of a green and white gas station sign and gasped. "We're in Crozet?! How long have I been asleep?" I dabbed the corners of my mouth to be sure I hadn't been drooling.

"About a half hour. I took the long way around, figured we could get a latte and a cookie and then go to Mint Springs Playground."

The sheriff had said the magic words "Mint Springs" and "playground." "Playground, Mommy. Let's go to a playground!" Sawyer was straining against the straps of his car seat.

"You sure?" I said to Santiago. "He's not an easy one to get back into that seat once he's got slides and monkey bars at hand."

"I wouldn't have said anything if I wasn't sure." He winked at me and parked in front of the Mudhouse. "Just don't tell the barista in Octonia that I visited the competition."

"I'm fairly sure that forty-five-minutes distance eliminates the threat of this being their competition," I said with a laugh.

Santiago gave me a serious stare. "You'd be surprised." Then he opened the back door and asked Sawyer if he could take him out of his car seat.

To my utter surprise, my "Mama Only" son said, "Yes, Mr. Policeman" and not only let Santiago take him out of the seat but held his hand to walk inside. The two of them were so darn cute and deeply enrapt in a conversation about trains that I took it upon myself to order us two lattes, with decaf espresso, and a chocolate chip cookie.

When I came back, Sawyer had his little hand up and was making the train whistle sound as he pumped his arm. Just then a train came by on the raised tracks outside the window, and both Santiago and Sawyer pressed their faces against the glass with glee.

The train was a long one, loaded with tractor trailers that baffled Sawyer. "There's truck on the train," he kept saying. I watched my son's joy and admired the man who had thought enough to share it with him . . . and found myself hopeful.

Sawyer's father and I had split about a year ago. It had been a hard few months figuring out custody arrangements and moving first to an apartment and then to our farmhouse. But finally, we'd hit a rhythm, and I could see my son's full self shining like I hadn't seen it since he was an infant, before his dad and I started feeling the tension of our marriage weighing us all down.

I wasn't much interested in dating, still had some healing to do, some figuring out the part of me that had made things hard in my marriage. Plus, single parenting a toddler for most hours of the week was exhausting enough that in the hours Saw was with his dad, I only caught up on work and then just stitched and watched TV.

But this moment right here, well, it made me wonder if maybe, just maybe I might think about letting a man into my life again, especially if he could bring my son this much delight.

True to form, though, Sawyer disrupted my contemplative moment with the pronouncement of "I have to poop" and sent me scrambling to find the bathroom. Twenty minutes later, we were back at the table – it's a long process when you're two and half – and Santiago had wisely gotten us to-go cups and a bag for Saw's cookie. Soon, we were back in the patrol car and on our way to the playground.

Sawyer went head-first down the twisty slide, and then he was off playing and talking with two other preschoolers while Santiago and I took a bench that looked out past the playground over the pond and the mountains beyond.

The silence of the afternoon settled over us, punctuated only by the squeals of children playing, and I was loath to disrupt it. Still, I had a question about the Scruggs store, and I knew Santiago might have some thoughts. "Do you think Luther Angelis's and Bailey Thomas's murders are connected?"

He tilted his head and then turned to look at me. "I do. Coincidences don't just happen like that." He looked back out over the water. "Your question makes me think you have a theory about that, too?"

I sighed. "I really don't want to have a theory. I'm not interested in doing police work, but given what you told me about the marijuana and Davison's appearance at the store . . . and the money, it seems like they are." I felt a lump rise in my throat. "And that makes me sad, honestly. I really wanted to be able to tell Berlinda and George only good things about their family's history in that place."

Santiago reached over and squeezed my hand before letting it go again. I missed the warmth of his fingers immediately. "I can understand that," he said. "But given that they let the building fall into its present condition after Luther's murder, I'd say they already feel the story is tainted."

"True," I said with a shrug, "but until recently, it seemed like Luther's murder was random, or at least not connected to anything he was doing."

A smile teased the sheriff's lips. "You know that most murders happen because the victim was involved with the murderer, often in less than savory ways, right?"

I thought about his statement and nodded. "So what you're saying is that there aren't serial killers looking to randomly murder people on every corner despite what TV would have me believe?"

"Precisely. Still, we don't know that Luther Angelis was involved with anything unsavory." He looked at me out of the corner of his eye.

"But someone was." I let out a hard breath.

"Yes, someone was," the sheriff said as he jumped up to push Sawyer on the swing.

AN HOUR LATER, as I loaded Sawyer into the car seat for the ride home, I decided to be bold and do something I almost never did: ask for help. "Santiago, would you be willing to drive back through town and let me pick up my dad's van so I can get all those cases of soda out of your office?"

"Sure," he said as I climbed into the passenger seat. "Just tell me where I'm going."

As soon as we headed toward Dad and Lucille's house, I regretted the suggestion, not because I thought Santiago minded but because I knew my dad and stepmom would definitely take note of this man bringing me by, a man I was going to let drive off with my son in his car. I was never going to hear the end of this.

8

Fortunately, my father and Lucille were on their best behavior, and Santiago was a real charmer, even offering to help my dad with a fencing project at our farmhouse when Dad mentioned what he was up to in terms of projects.

"I'm a master with a fence puller," the sheriff said, and I could almost see my dad swoon.

It was only when we were leaving and Sawyer let Santiago strap him into his car seat again that Lucille leaned over to whisper, "Va Va Voom, Pais. You go, girl."

The blush on my face could probably have set the sun afire, but fortunately, Lucille distracted Santiago by handing him a cake carrier and saying, "Pumpkin cake with cream cheese frosting. For the department."

Santiago beamed and immediately put the cake carrier on the car, took off the lid, and ran his finger through the frosting on half of the cake. "Delicious!" he said as he licked his finger.

"Smart man," Lucille said with a laugh. "Way to claim your portion."

He winked at her and got in. "See you two at the station," he said as he pumped the siren. I could hear Sawyer's laughter all the way through the closed windows.

Dad had offered to come along so that he could drive the van to my house and save a trip for one of us. His presence was going to be a big help, but I also knew he was hoping to "have a conversation" with his only daughter.

Sure enough, we hadn't even made it out of their neighborhood when he said, "So now you and the sheriff are taking road trips? I thought I warned you about this." His voice wasn't harsh, but he was very serious.

I racked my brain, trying to think about what exactly my dad, who never talked about relationships with me, might have said to warn me about dating the sheriff. I couldn't come up with anything, but fortunately, Dad clarified quickly.

"You really, really don't want to get involved in police business, Paisley. It's dangerous, and you don't really know what you're doing."

I took a long, deep breath, mostly to keep from laughing, before I said, "I'm not getting involved with police business, Daddy." Then, somehow, the next sentence just poured forth like I had no control over my own mouth. "I may be getting involved with a police officer, though."

Now, it was my dad's turn to be baffled. Out of the corner of my eye, I could see he was staring straight ahead with his forehead folded as fully as it could be. "You're dating the sheriff?" he finally asked.

For the four hundred millionth time that day, I blushed. "Not exactly. I mean, I don't know. Not yet. Maybe." I let out a long sigh. "Maybe."

A smile slowly crept up my dad's face and unfolded his forehead. "Good for you, Baby Girl," he said as he squeezed my hands. "Good for you."

We rode the next few minutes in silence, but then I decided to take advantage of having my dad to myself and ask him a few questions. "Dad, did you ever hear of someone growing pot up by Scruggs Store?"

I could tell by my dad's lack of reaction that I hadn't surprised him. My dad wasn't exactly one of the good old boys of Octonia County, but he knew a lot of things, often because people underestimated him. His good nature and deafness made people think he was stupid or unobservant. My dad was neither.

"I may have. Why do you ask?"

I told Dad about how the stand was still thriving and had obviously been cared for over a long time.

"Makes sense. A couple folks I knew who track native plants for the state ran across the stand a few years back. They decided not to report it to the authorities because they are of the 'live and let live' sort when it comes to plants, except invasive species." He chuckled. "If it had been a stand of Tree of Heaven, though, they would have been out there with chainsaws themselves."

I joined my dad in laughing. Dad was passionate about plants, including native species, but he found fanaticism about anything, including his beloved trees, to be frustrating. We'd shared many an inside joke about the people who lost their mind over the way kudzu took over swaths of the Virginia countryside but saw no danger in their own wisteria vines or English Ivy, despite the fact that these species spread like wildfire and were just as hard to eradicate as kudzu.

"So it's possible the stand has been there for more than two years?"

Dad thought for a moment and then said, "Probably. Seems like my friend found the stand ten or fifteen years back." He shrugged. Clearly this was not his top priority in terms of plant issues.

We finished the ride by chatting about Sawyer's latest escapades of climbing, which included scaling the interior of the small barn at the farmhouse. I'd had to coax him down with the promise of a lollipop *and* a marshmallow while I stood below him hoping that by placing my body under his, I'd break his fall and still be conscious and able to call 911 for help with my own injuries.

When we pulled up at the sheriff's office, Sawyer and Santiago were already out front, and Saw was holding a case of soda. He was clearly at the limits of his strength, but I could see him struggling to hold on to the Cheerwine box so that I could see him. I jumped out and said, "Sawyer Sutton, you are so strong!! Wow!!"

At that point, he let go of the box, and I cringed as I imagined my small profits pouring down the sidewalk. Fortunately, Santiago was quick and caught the box and set it down as Sawyer sprinted to hug me.

"Mama, I got to run the siren up the highway," he said as he let me scoop him up. "It was super loud."

I laughed. "I bet all the cars moved out of your way?"

"They did. They were scared of me." He grinned and jumped down to dodge around his Boppy's legs.

"That was really kind of you," I said to Santiago as he began carrying cases of soda to the van.

"It's kind of fun for me, too. I don't usually get to use that thing unless there's an emergency." He leaned toward me and mock-whispered, "Just don't tell the boss."

"Oh no," I said as my hand flew to my mouth. "I think he already knows."

Within a few minutes we had everything loaded, including Sawyer in his car seat in my car. Only the promise of ice cream convinced him that the police cruiser wasn't his ideal ride home.

Dad headed off toward my house with the van full, and I lingered outside my car, not sure how to thank Santiago for the afternoon. I decided simple was best. "Thank you."

He smiled. "You're welcome. And maybe sometime, your dad can watch Sawyer, and we can do dinner?"

I ducked my head and blushed, yet again, but nodded. "I'd like that," I said before I climbed into the car and felt panic begin to rise. I really liked Santiago, but I wasn't sure I was ready. I tried to smile as I drove off, but I probably grimaced instead.

BY THE TIME we got home, Dad had already begun unloading the cases into the creamery at the back of the farmhouse. Sawyer had insisted since the day we moved in that the big concrete basin that had been used for keeping milk and cream cool was a bathtub, and I knew one day I'd find him back there naked with a hose. For now, though, it was protected from the weather, and until it got cold enough to freeze the drinks, I could store them there. Hopefully by the time we were getting that cold, I'd have sold the merchandise and could soon afford to insulate and run electricity out there to make it a proper storage room.

While Dad and I unloaded the rest, Sawyer scampered around the yard attempting to climb forty-foot cherry trees and threatening to scale the barn walls again. Fortunately, Dad had helped me out by stapling chicken wire along the exposed beams just so I wouldn't have to act as a human airbag should my son scale the walls like a monkey again.

I left the back door open so I could hear Saw playing and invited Dad in for hot chocolate. "Be in in just a sec. I want to grab something," he said.

It was just getting cold enough to enjoy my favorite warm beverages, and I knew Dad was a sucker for hot chocolate made with milk and a heap of tiny marshmallows. I knew this because both his daughter and his grandson liked the same.

Dad came in and headed for the couch in the living room,

displacing Beauregard unceremoniously from his blanket on one side of the loveseat. I carried our drinks in on a small tray and set them on the antique trunk I used as a coffee table, and then I noticed the piece of countertop on Dad's knees. "Interesting piece, isn't it?"

"It is." Dad held it up in front of him. "I expect you picked it up for the ads, but did you see this?" He pointed to a column of numbers on the underside of the board. I was surprised Santiago and I hadn't noticed those when we saw the note to Mary, but then, I'd been so enthralled with that find that it hadn't even occurred to me to look for anything further.

I took the board from Dad and held it up to the dwindling sunlight coming through the window and then made my way over to my office lamp and clicked it on. "It looks like a tally of some sort. Four digits followed by a period and two digits. Dollars and cents?"

"That's what I was thinking," Dad said. "But underneath the counter where no one would see it?"

I sat down and studied the numbers. Each entry was for a few thousand dollars. I peered more closely at the column and saw, to the left of it a series of four-digit numbers written in the same hand. "Look, Dad. What do those look like to you?"

He stood and came to peer over my shoulder. "It's hard for me to see, but are you talking about those years written beside the dollar figures?"

"Exactly," I said. There, written clear as day were the numbers from 1922 to 1999. I let my shoulders fall back against the chair. "These are the years that correspond with these figures." I was aching to call Santiago and tell him what we'd found, but I couldn't do that with Dad here.

But I couldn't ask Dad to leave because we'd just sat down with our drinks. It would have to wait . . . and I hated waiting.

Still, I pushed myself to focus on my dad, talking with him about his volunteer work and the latest baking escapades that

Lucille was undertaking. "I've had to start skipping lunch just so that I can eat some of what she bakes for me at eleven p.m. If I didn't, I'd have to get all new clothes."

I smiled. Lucille was a very good baker, and since my dad wore shirts until they basically disintegrated on his skin, I didn't think there was any real risk that he'd be seeking out a new wardrobe anytime soon, even if he did gain a few pounds.

After a brief chat, though, Dad was ready to go. He wasn't a man for small talk, and I wasn't able to think of a substantial discussion point for us just then. We headed out to find Saw, who was waist-deep in the field next door and waving a stick over his head saying, "Go away, Werewolf." No werewolf was going to mess with him, that's for sure.

Beckoned over by that ice cream I'd promised, Saw trotted across the field to the porch so that Dad could give him a hug before pulling out off toward home. Just then, a freight train rumbled by on the other side of our driveway. Some people might think that having a train basically in your yard was a problem. Not Sawyer and me. We loved it, and we were getting to know the conductors, too. Tonight, the man in the engine was the older, black gentleman who frequently did the runs with the longest trains. Once Sawyer and I had counted over a hundred and eighty cars behind his engine.

Sawyer had already sprinted to the fence as the train approached, and now he was pumping his arm fiercely to get the whistle to blow. He was rewarded soon after with a long whistle and then two short ones, the sound I'd come to think of as our "train ringtone."

Once the train had passed, Sawyer meandered inside to look for "his cat." Beauregard put up with Sawyer with about as much patience as one could expect from a cat, and tonight, all rested up from a day at home, he tolerated quite a bit of snuggling while I made us tomato soup and grilled cheese sandwiches followed by mint chocolate chip ice cream, my favorite and Saw's, too. But then any ice cream was Sawyer's favorite. After dinner, Saw busied himself with a toy ship Mika had given him a few months ago.

I took the chance to text Santiago about the makeshift ledger on the board, and he got back to me right away. *Can you send a picture?*

I snapped one and read his almost instant response. *Notice the final figure there.*

The board fit easily on my kitchen counter, so I flipped on the lights and studied it more closely. Then, suddenly, like a bolt of understanding, I saw what Santiago had noticed immediately. *The dollar figures match!!!!* I added as many exclamation points as I thought reasonable for a grown woman.

You've just found the ledger for the cash stash at the store, Paisley.

Does it mean something that we have this now? I replied.

It might, he said.

I waited for him to say more, but then I heard a knock on my front door. "You're quick," I said when I looked out the glass to see him on our side porch.

"Still on duty for a few hours." He peeked in but couldn't see Sawyer. "I don't have to come in if it'll make it harder for Sawyer to begin to settle for bed."

My heart fluttered a little at his thoughtfulness. "Actually, it might get him riled up. Do you mind if I just bring you the counter piece? Then, after I get him settled, we can chat." I smiled. "I mean, if you're on duty that late."

"I am. The next shift starts at ten. Unless your toddler is a night owl."

"Good gracious, no, not if I can help it." I glanced at the clock on the stove. "He should be down by eight-thirty. Come in for some hot tea then?"

He nodded and took the board out of my hands. As he

turned to go, I said, "Thanks for staying back a bit while Dad was here. I don't want him to worry."

"I figured," the sheriff said with a wink. "See you soon."

Sawyer gave me a run for my money at bedtime, but given that he bolted around the house for twenty minutes solid before I could get him to lay down, his resistance was mostly spent by the time he was prone. He was out in five minutes flat, and I slipped downstairs and flashed the outside light. I figured that would be enough signal for the sheriff.

Sure enough, in a few moments, he was at the door and then on the stool beside me at the kitchen counter. He had brought the counter piece back in, and we laid it across mine. "Do you mind if I take some more pictures?" he asked.

I laughed. "You're asking me for permission to take images of something I salvaged from a crime scene?"

"I try to be courteous," he said as he snapped away. Then he bent close over the board. "You saw the dates, right?"

"I did." I'd pulled out my notebook and compared the dates on the board to the dates of the Scruggs family. "Looks like Alice started putting money away back when she first inherited the store."

"Looks like it." He pointed to the first figure. "She managed to save $85.16 this first year. That's like three weeks' wages in that time."

I stared at him. "And you just happened to know that?"

"No," he rolled his eyes. "I Googled. Thanks for the Wi-Fi passwords, by the way."

I smiled and sat down to study the numbers. "There's cash put in every year until 1999 when the store was abandoned."

I stopped and pondered the board before grabbing my laptop. I opened the Scruggs family tree and saw what I thought may have been the case: Sheila Scruggs died in 1996, three years before her son. I spun the laptop around so Santiago could see it and pointed to Sheila's death date. "So

Luther was the only one who knew the money was there, and when he died . . ."

"The secret in the cabinet died with him." The sheriff leaned back and studied the ceiling for a minute. "Doesn't it seem odd to you that Berlinda Jefferson had nothing to do with the store? I mean it was her inheritance, too, right?"

I sighed. "Yeah, I guess so." I opened my phone photo app and scanned through the images of the Scruggs wills that I'd taken the other day, then turned the laptop to face Santiago. "Sheila did leave the store to both of them. Berlinda wasn't interested though. That's what she told me." I pulled my laptop back over. "Plus, she was actually married by the time she inherited the store. Makes sense that she didn't want to be tied to those hours and all that hard work."

"Did they grow up in the store?" The sheriff asked as he studied the countertop again.

"No, they lived closer to town. Berlinda told me that her mom hired someone to run the store while she was a school-teacher." I frowned and studied the screen. "Still, you'd think her mother would have told her about the money?"

I ran my fingers down the column of years. When Sheila Angelis died in 1996, there was over $90,000 in that cabinet.

The sheriff followed my finger and cleared his throat. "Does seem odd," he said as he stood up. "I'll look into this more. Thanks for telling me about it." His voice was distant, distracted.

"Sure. I wouldn't want to hold anything back from you, from the police, I mean." I stood up and carried our mugs to the sink to cover my embarrassment. But when I turned around, Santiago was already heading out the door. "See you later?"

He was almost all the way onto the porch when he turned back with a small smile. "I sure hope so," he said. I could hear him on the phone as he walked to the car. Something definitely had gotten into his craw about our conversation.

I brewed myself another cup of tea and sat down on the couch with Jonatha Brooke playing softly on my laptop beside me. I needed music to soothe me, but I also wanted the space to think.

We had a stash of cash that no one, even the people living in the house, knew about, a stand of marijuana that had been growing for years, and two murders. It felt like these things had to be connected somehow.

But no matter how many stitches of the central carousel horse I put in place, I couldn't tie the threads of history together. Eventually, I turned off the music, stashed my sewing, and went to bed to let my subconscious weave the picture together.

THE NEXT MORNING, when an exuberant toddler popped up from where he'd settled in my bed at about 3:13 a.m. and said, "Time to get up," I had no more clarity about the story of the Scruggs store. But I did have the first line of my story for the newsletter, and that felt like victory enough for the morning.

Before I could sit down to write, though, Sawyer needed clothes and some bacon, and I needed a shower. I got the toddler dressed and set up with his iPad and *Bob the Builder* and jumped into the shower, which I was able to enjoy for a full five minutes before the shouts of "Mama" echoed through the house. Still, I did manage to rinse my hair, so I counted that the second win of the day.

When Saw ate his bacon, I knew I was on a roll and packed him and Beauregard up for a ride to Saw's dad's house. I said goodbye to Sawyer as he sprinted to the sandbox and managed to keep my tears in until I got out of the driveway. It was always so hard to say goodbye, but I knew I needed the break for my mental health and our finances, too. I let myself cry a few minutes and then put on some loud music and danced my way downtown.

Mika and I had come to an arrangement for our Saturdays. I'd do my writing at the store, let Beauregard draw tourists in with his girth and glory in the window, and help out with her customer rushes . . . and she'd keep me caffeinated and on task. By ten a.m., I had picked up chocolate croissants for both of us from the new bakery in town and was sitting in one of her wingback chairs with my laptop.

"The legacy of the Scruggs Store is one of dedication, determination, and devotion." It wasn't the most captivating of opening lines, but I figured that my readers would appreciate the sentiment. And I'd already hooked them on the history, of course, since they were already subscribers. This wasn't some clickbait on social media after all.

The rest of the story of the store poured out of me, from Alice's original inheritance to Sheila being raised there to Luther taking over for his mom and grandmother and moving back into the house at the rear. It was a story of family strength as well as the tale of a beloved community institution. I had the article written within the hour, and I was thrilled to include a couple photos: the one of Alice and Sheila and a close-up of the top of the countertop with the advertisements featured prominently. I made sure to not show any of the words about the cabinet or the ledger on the back of the board because I wanted to be very careful to keep my word to Santiago about not revealing anything pertinent to the investigation.

Then, I uploaded the images of the various, salvaged items, which I'd snapped quickly this morning while Sawyer played in the yard, and created listings for everything but the counter – since it might still need to be evidence and could benefit from a coat of poly anyway – on my favorite online auction site.

Finally, in my newsletter, I added a photo and a link to each of the items and scheduled the article to go out at one p.m.

My work for the day done and the store business still well-in-hand by Mika, who had hydrated me and managed the steady stream of customers without any assistance for two hours, I started my usual work of straightening the yarn and "shelf enhancers," a term Mika had taken from Ellery Adams' Secret, Book, and Scone society mysteries, around the store.

I had a system. I started in the back and organized all the yarn in its bins while also moving tchotchkes like candlesticks in the shape of huskies and owl bookends made of cast iron to the place they felt like they most aligned with the yarn. Today, I paired a beautiful copper pie tin with an orange and gold sari yarn and set a beautiful blue glass bud vase against a bin of magenta alpaca yarn.

Mika swore by my system and said she sold more yarn and more whatnots on Saturdays than any other day of the week. I took the compliment and didn't point out that this was also her busiest day of the week.

Between batches of sorting, I scanned the photos of my inventory of items in the garage to see what I might bring over for Mika to consider selling. We had long ago decided to help one another out without obligation. If I found something I thought she might like, I'd salvage it, share it with her when it seemed appropriate, and sell it to her at a small mark-up if she wanted to add it to her store. If she thought of something or had a customer ask for something she'd like to carry, she'd let me know to be on the lookout. The arrangement didn't make either of us millionaires, but it did bring us each a little extra cash that could be legitimately written off come tax time. More importantly, it let us support each other's businesses without putting either of us in financial peril.

I was straightening the bins right at the front of the store and had dumped a pile of pastel cotton yarn on one of the chairs to sort it by color and put it back in its crate with a sense of order when I heard the front door of the shop open. Since Mika was free, I didn't even look up. But a minute later, I felt a presence standing over me and looked up to see the face of the man who had been on the Scruggs store porch looking at me from about two feet away.

He didn't look like he was here to pick up some yarn for his latest scarf project. He was glaring right at me.

I smiled, belatedly, and then said, "Hello. Can I help you?" I decided it was best to play dumb. He couldn't know I knew he was Victor Davison, so I hoped I could play the part.

"You know me," he said in a low, gravelly voice that resembled the growl of a bear.

"I'm sorry. I don't think I do." Clearly, my plan was not going to work, but I decided to milk the moment of confusion for as long as I could. I scooped up all the yarn I had been sorting and dumped it into the crate before holding the box in front of me like some sort of squishy, soft shield. "Should I?"

"Yes."

I waited for him to say more, but when he just stood glaring, I glanced over his shoulder and saw Mika with her phone under her chin and her fingers flashing the numbers 9-1-1. I felt a measure better but knew I had to keep this situation under control. "Okay, then. Where should I know you from?" I tried to look casual as I stepped back and sideways to put the bin back on the shelf and shift so that the chair was between us. "The grocery store maybe? The library?"

A low sound came from the man's throat.

"I'm sorry. I didn't catch that," I said, hoping I sounded sincere and not just stupid.

"You saw me down at Luther's old store," he finally said.

I tilted my head and tried to act like I was figuring out what he meant. Finally, I said, "Oh, you mean the Scruggs store south of town? Oh yes, I've been salvaging there, but I didn't see you there." I hated to lie, but if it meant not being hurt . . . "Are you with the police? Did you come when I found that poor woman's body?" Now I was really pressing it, but I had to stall . . . and short of saying, "Oh, you're the guy growing pot behind the building," this was the only way I thought I could suggest we had met.

Davison stepped around the chair toward me, and I took several steps back, right into the window ledge. I was out of room to run.

"You know about it." Davison stepped further forward, and I leaned back and thought about jumping up into the display itself. At least, I fleetingly considered, I could find something to throw and break the window out to run.

Fortunately, I didn't have to risk glass cuts or a massive bill to cover for Mika because just then Beauregard leaped over my shoulder and right onto Davison's chest. He sunk his claws into the flannel of the man's shirt and hung on.

Davison flailed and tried to knock my giant cat off his chest, but Beau just scaled his chest and planted four sets of claws into his shoulders, where Davison couldn't reach him. I took the chance to run toward Mika, and as soon as Beau saw I was clear, he leapt off and followed Mika and me to the front door. We sprinted out onto the sidewalk, and I ran smack dab into Santiago's chest.

He pulled me off his body, looked in my face, nodded, and then pushed me aside as he stepped in front of Davison as he barreled out the front door. Despite the fact that he was fifty pounds lighter than Davison, the sheriff stood his ground and said, "Stop. Police. What is going on here?"

Davison looked at the sheriff in his full uniform and let out a long sigh. "Nothing, Officer. I just wanted to talk to Ms. Sutton here, but then her kitty attacked me."

I bent down and scooped up Beauregard and whispered,

"Good boy." His purr rose up solid and loud in his chest as he rubbed his chin against my fingers.

Santiago looked at me. "Did you order your cat to attack this man?" I could see the smile in his eyes.

"I did not. I have never been able to get this cat to do anything on command. He is, after all, a cat." I could feel myself starting to shake after the fright, but I burrowed my fingers further into Beau's fur to steady myself.

"Mika, did you hear any command given for the cat to attack?" The sheriff asked Mika, who stood beside me with her hands on her hips. If looks could kill, Davison would have dropped dead right there.

"I did not. What I did see was this man advancing on Paisley in my store. I won't press charges, but I would like him to leave." Mika's jaw was clenched, and she looked angry enough to follow Beau's lead and attack Davison.

"Sir, clearly this is a misunderstanding. If you'd like we can talk about it down at the station." Santiago's voice was completely serious.

Davison said, "No. I'm leaving." He charged around the three of us and stomped down the sidewalk toward a beat-up green pickup truck with the long handles of tools sticking out of the back.

I squeezed Beau tight as I watched Davison's truck roll down the street. Then, I turned to Santiago and said, "Thank you. You were just in time."

"Thank your friend there," he said with a nod toward Mika. "She's the one who called and told me someone was threatening you."

I turned to Mika and hugged her, squishing Beau between us, a fact that he seemed to love and hate in equal measure. "Thank you for thinking fast."

Mika smiled and then held the door open for Santiago and me. We headed toward the chairs at the front, and Mika unfolded another seat for the sheriff before dropping into the wingback across from me. "Man, that was terrifying," she said as she tucked her arms around her torso.

"It looked scary from what I saw," the sheriff said. "What did he want?"

I gave Beauregard a good rubdown before laying out my jacket in the window ledge and setting him on it. I planned to give him a can of tuna later as a reward. When I sat back down, I shrugged. "I honestly have no idea. He seemed to want me to acknowledge I knew who he was, but I don't know why. He just glowered and cornered me."

"Sounds like he was trying to intimidate you, scare you off," Santiago said with a frown.

"Well, he did intimidate me, and I am scared . . . but off of what? I'm not a threat to him." My brain was a little fuzzy as the adrenaline wore off, so I knew I might have been missing something.

Santiago put his hand on my arm, and I felt Mika's eyes catch that little movement like she was a honey trap and the gesture was a fly. "You haven't been back to the store have you?"

"You know I haven't," I said flatly and watched Mika's eyes grow wide. I hadn't told her I was under police protection, so there's no telling what she thought of that comment. But from the smile on her face, it looked like she was enjoying her thoughts.

Santiago shook his head. "We must be missing something. Clearly, he thinks you know more than you do. Glad we were close by."

"We?" Mika asked.

I sighed. "I've been under police protection for a few days now." I explained how the murder had been committed while I was at the store and how the sheriff's office had thought it best that they stay close.

Mika nodded and then her expression turned to a scowl.

"So how come you didn't come without me having to call today?" I could tell she was trying to keep her tone light, but the accusation came through loud and clear.

Santiago cleared his throat and looked at the floor. "The deputy was, er, indisposed."

I laughed so loudly that Beauregard jumped. "So I was nearly assaulted because someone had to take a pee break?! That's perfect." I doubled over in mirth. "I've always wondered about that in those stakeouts on TV," I said between laughs.

"Especially if the officers are women," Mika said as the post-confrontation relief hit her with giggles. "The pee in a bottle trick doesn't work as well for us."

Santiago didn't succumb to the hysteria like we did, but he did smile and sit patiently while we laughed out the last of our fear. Then he said, "Well, we're going to keep a closer eye on Davison now. That's for certain." He stood and headed toward the door.

"I'll let the deputy on duty know what transpired, but Paisley, please give Mika my cell number. Both of you call anytime, okay?" He winked at me and went out the door.

I tried to turn away and go back to the bin of pastel yarn that I'd basically thrown into place, but Mika grabbed my arm and said, "Oh no you don't. You and the sheriff?"

My shrug was half-hearted at best, and within a minute, I was sitting down and telling her about the coffee dates and the drive with him the day before. "I just don't know if I'm ready, Miks." Tears welled up in my eyes.

"Then, wait until you do know. That man, if my romance Spidey-sense is still keen, is way into you and wouldn't want you to do anything until you were sure. He'll wait, or he won't. And if he doesn't, then it's his loss." Mika blew me a kiss and wandered to the other side of the store to help a customer pick out yarn for an afghan.

I began to re-sort the pinks from the light greens from the

baby blues and yellows. Like cross-stitch, organizing yarn felt calming. It gave me room to think while also giving my body something to do. I wondered if this was why all those knitters and crocheters had those huge yarn stashes – was it therapeutic just to organize them?

I finished that bin and made my way to the final crate of the day – my favorite. Alpaca yarn. I have always had a dream of owning alpacas, and once Sawyer and I were more financially stable, I had a plan to fence off the lower part of our property and put the run-in shed there to use for a couple of those beauties, maybe the ones that were retiring from the competition circuit. Mika knew how to clean, card, and spin fiber, so I figured she could make use of their coats when I had them sheared in late spring. As I sorted the muted blues and browns of the bin, I let my mind travel down that dream for a while.

Finally, with the store all sorted and the end of the day looming near, I settled into one of Mika's chairs to stitch and think. For days like this, I brought along small projects – this time, I was working on a scarecrow with some crows and pumpkins from my favorite Etsy shop for cute patterns, NonStopStitch. The pattern was simple and straightforward, so good for quick sessions on the go.

I had just finished stitching the white pumpkin at the bottom of the design when a familiar voice said my name. I looked up to see Berlinda Jefferson smiling at me. "I didn't know you did cross-stitch," she said as she looked over the top of my small hoop.

I tucked my needle into the fabric and stood up to hug her. "It's my favorite hobby. Relaxes me and gives me time to think."

"I hear that. I do jigsaw puzzles for the same reason." She squeezed my arm. "But today, I'm looking for yarn. I have a friend who is ill, and while I should be the one making something for her, she insists that crochet is the one thing she wants to do when she's stuck in bed."

I lifted my chin and said, "But don't you have yarn stores in Richmond?" I glanced over at Mika who was smiling at me. "I mean this one is the best in the State, but—"

Mika cleared her throat.

I smiled. "I mean, this is the best one in the country. But surely there's one closer to you," I finished.

Berlinda shrugged. "Oh, there are, but any excuse we have to come back, we take it. George was especially keen to come over today, and I never pass up a chance to come home." She looked around. "And I love this store. So cozy, and all these knick-knacks are so winsome."

I grinned. "Where is George?" I peeked out the door to see if he might be waiting in the car.

"He's up the street at the microbrewery. Yarn didn't interest him, but their new pumpkin ale did." She laughed.

"I hear that. Mika, burgers and pumpkin ale after close?"

"You know it," she said and headed toward the storeroom to get her backstock and fill in the holes now visible from my organizing and from the massive yarn purchase the afghan-maker had made from her heavy-weight yarn.

"Have time to sit?" I asked and pointed at the other chair.

"Sure, for a minute. I was hoping to run into you anyway," she said.

I smiled, but inwardly, I paused, nervous about exactly why she wanted to see me. "Glad you found me then."

Berlinda smiled thinly and said, "I actually wanted to ask you not to send out the article about my grandmother, not yet anyway." She winced as if expecting me to object.

"Oh no," I said as I looked at the time on my phone. "The email went out about three hours ago. I'm sorry. I didn't realize—"

A wash of something that looked like fear spread over Berlinda's face for a quick second before she smiled again and waved a hand. "Not a big deal. I just didn't want anyone getting the wrong idea what with poor Bailey's murder and all."

I looked at her a minute and tried to figure out what wrong idea she thought people might get. "What are you worried people might think, Berlinda?"

"Oh, I'm probably being a little too concerned, but I don't want people gossiping that we were trying to take advantage of the interest in our store, you know, now that we've decided not to tear it down."

"What?! You're not demolishing it after all. What brought about that change of heart?" I was trying to think about what I would do if people had already started bidding on the things I'd salvaged. It would ruin my reputation if I couldn't fulfill the orders.

Berlinda must have read my mind though because she said, "Don't worry, dear. Nothing you salvaged is important. You can keep it all." She smiled and then studied the back of her hands. "I just couldn't do it. After talking with you and thinking about what my family had built there, I just couldn't tear it down."

I nodded. I loved every old building I went into, and none of them were buildings my family had owned for generations. I couldn't imagine what that felt like. "I totally get that," I said.

"So I decided to use the money," she lowered her voice a bit, "the sheriff found and fix the building up. Make it a convenience store again."

I clapped with delight. "I love that idea. There's nothing down that way, and I for one would love to have a place to grab a gallon of milk when I don't feel like driving to town."

"That's what I was thinking, too. Plus, if the county approves, we'll put in new gas tanks and sell fuel, too. Maybe even open the kitchen back up for breakfast and lunch." She was glowing even as she talked. She looked like a woman who had made a decision that was bringing her peace.

"Well, you know I'll fill up at your pumps, Berlinda. I love this. When do you plan to start work?" I was envisioning an article in the local paper if the editor would let me freelance one, a history of the store combined with a grand opening announcement.

"We have to wait until the investigation is closed, but hopefully by the beginning of the new year." She smiled but then grew serious. "So you don't think people will think ill of us?"

I shook my head. "Nope, most people wouldn't think that no matter what I wrote, but I only focused on the history of the building and the objects I found there. Nothing current, so if anyone is going to be accused of taking advantage, it'll be me."

Berlinda smiled. "Well, let's hope that people are just happy to learn, for both our sakes. Glad I found you then. And thank you, Paisley. You inspired me." She stood and walked over to my chair. "I think you may have saved my family's story, Paisley."

I felt tears prick my eyes and stood quickly to avoid crying. "Oh, the story would have still been there, Berlinda, but I'm glad the building that goes with it will remain, too." I walked her to Mika, who was waiting to help with the yarn part of Berlinda's visit. "You'll let me know if I can help?"

"Will do, and I do think I'll need a certain bench maker to come by and help us with some outdoor furnishings. I hope to have live music in the summer." She smiled.

"Oh, Sawyer is definitely up for the challenge." I laughed. "I'm his mother, so I can volunteer him."

After she picked up a dozen skeins of a gorgeous deep purple yarn, I watched Berlinda walk down the street and smiled. My two unexpected visits today couldn't have been more different, and yet I found myself unsettled by both. Davison's confrontation was obviously off-putting, but something about the fact that Berlinda was going to restore the store was also troubling me. I couldn't figure out quite what, though, and I decided to stop borrowing trouble and enjoy a beer and a burger with my best friend instead.

. . .

THE WALK to the brewery was brief and crisp, and I savored every lungful of autumn air. I loved things about every season, but if I had to pick only one, it would be fall, a fall evening particularly. The encroaching darkness, the cool temperatures, the colors in the trees – they all spoke of the things I loved best: a cozy home, a quiet place, and the grandeur of nature all around.

Still, I welcomed the pressure of warm air on my face as we walked into the clattering cavern of the microbrewery. It had been constructed in an old plastic-manufacturing plant, so it had this funky charm that was half old-world and half super-contemporary with abstract glass pendants dangling beside the huge, silver ductwork. I had only been here a couple of times since they opened a little over a year ago because it wasn't exactly the best place to bring a toddler who, five out of ten times, would still throw his food rather than eat it. But I was glad to be there now.

Mika pointed to a tall table in a back corner away from the kitchen and the TV screen showing some sort of event with a ball. I nodded and followed her through the fans of whatever had just happened with said ball. Sports were great to watch live because of the energy of the crowd and, well, because of the stadium food. But the sport itself . . . I could take or leave. Still, it was fun to see people enjoying something, as long as they didn't expect me to enjoy it with them.

We climbed up onto our stools and immediately took a look at the beer menu. I had that pumpkin ale Berlinda had mentioned on my mind, but I decided, instead, to go with something I rarely treated myself to, a chocolate stout. The ABV was high, so I would have to take it slow and be sure to eat . . . and even then, I might have to camp out for a couple of hours on Mika's sofa, but it was worth it to taste that bitter chocolate-ish goodness.

Mika got some IPA that I declined to even try because I could not stand the taste of hops. I did, however, sample the appetizer of sweet potato fries that she ordered, and they were delicious. And when our burgers arrived stacked high with veggies and bacon and sharp, sharp cheddar, I felt myself relaxing in a way that I didn't often. Parenting a small child was so hard for me, even as I adored my son. I was someone who thrived on conversation and innovation, and parenting a toddler was made up of mostly repeating what Saw said and doing the same things over and over. I wouldn't trade it for the world, but I did look forward to when we could talk more . . . and when I could find a climbing harness that fit him so I could just suit him up in the morning, teach him how to hook a cara-biner to the rigging I was going to attach to every high object at the farmhouse, and watch him go.

Tonight, though, it was just about friendship and good food, and I didn't have to coax Mika to eat her tomato or tell her when to say excuse me. I did, however, have to put a morato-rium on talk of the sheriff and me. I had a lot I wanted to say there, but I wasn't ready to say it because, well, I didn't entirely know how I felt all the way.

"Totally get it," Mika said when I told her I'd rather talk about other things. "Tell me what was up with that Davison guy. Any ideas?"

I chomped down on my burger and suppressed a groan of pleasure at the crispness of the bacon and then sat back to think about what I could say without putting the case in jeop-ardy. I decided, almost instantly, I was going to tell her every-thing because, well, she was my best friend and because I needed to talk through things with someone who didn't short-circuit my brain synapses by being so charming.

"Well, he might be a murderer," I said. "Or just a drug dealer."

Mika slowly lowered her burger back to her plate without taking a bite. "Come again?"

I caught her up on Davison's visit to the store and on the pot situation, and then, with a deep breath, I said, "It's all really confusing because we found over a hundred thousand dollars in cash hidden in an old pie safe in the store."

This time, the woman nearly choked on a pickled carrot that was the house specialty. "Did you say over a hundred thousand dollars in a pie safe?"

I nodded. "But you cannot say anything about that to anyone. The sheriff knows, obviously, but no one else except the Jeffersons because the money belongs to them, of course."

Mika sat back and studied me for a minute. "It doesn't belong to the woman who lived there, the one you secretly questioned?"

"I didn't secretly question her," I said, far too defensively. "But no, apparently since the building was abandoned and Mary Johnson hadn't lived there in decades, it's the property of the owner." I took a sip of my stout and continued. "Besides, I don't think she even knew it was there. I mean, wouldn't you have taken the cash when you left if you knew it was there?"

Mika nodded but then paused and looked at her plate for a minute. "But what if she couldn't take it? I mean what if she wasn't allowed back in because it was a crime scene."

I pondered that a moment and decided it was a fair question for the sheriff when I next saw him. "But even if that was the case, wouldn't you have gone back eventually over the course of twenty years even if you had to sneak in?"

"I suppose," Mika said, "but didn't you say she and the Jeffersons didn't get along? Maybe she felt awkward going back."

"Is there any amount of awkward that would keep you from

going back for a hundred thousand dollars?" I asked with a raised eyebrow.

"Good point." She ate the last bite of her burger and then picked up her beer. "So do you think she might have finally gone back only to find Bailey Thomas there?"

I stared at my best friend because, well, I had never thought of that. It felt very unlikely that Mary Johnson would wait twenty years to go and get her money, but maybe she had thought it best to leave it where it was lest she should raise suspicion if she suddenly had a bunch of cash. "Like maybe since the building was about to be demolished, she thought this was her last chance."

Mika shrugged. "Something like that."

"It's a possibility." I added that idea to my mental checklist and said, "But it's also possible Davison killed Thomas because she found his pot operation."

"Could be, if he has a pot operation and if she knew about it." Mika picked up the table card that featured dessert and said, "Split Lucille's Pumpkin Bread Pudding with me?"

"Lucille's?" I took the card from her hand, and sure enough, there in the description it said, *Lucille's Bread Pudding is made by local baker, Lucille Nundrum.* "I had no idea she was baking professionally. Yes, let's get one." I wanted to order one of my own just to support Lucille, but this dinner was maxing out my dining budget for the week as it was. Mika caught the waiter's eye and ordered our bread pudding and two decaf coffees.

"It seems to me like you have two possibilities for who killed Bailey Thomas – Mary Johnson or Victor Davison. Or it could have been someone who had a beef with Bailey herself."

I sighed. "Yeah, I thought of that, but the sheriff has pursued that angle pretty hard, and while most of the town didn't like her, it doesn't seem like anyone disliked her enough to kill her."

Our bread pudding and coffee arrived, and I changed the

tack of the conversation. "When Berlinda was in your store earlier, she mentioned that she was going to use the money in the pie safe to refurbish the building. I love that . . ." my voice trailed off.

"You love it, but?" Mika said before shoveling a huge piece of pumpkin and bread soaked in cream and vanilla into her mouth.

"It just seems off somehow." I stretched and tried to get words around the tilted feeling I had about the whole thing. "The money gives them a reason to be able to do it now, but if you had any sense you wanted to keep the building, why plan to demolish it anyway? After all, it's been falling down for the better part of ten years. They could have torn the building down years ago, or they could have been saving to restore it. But it sounded like this was just out of the blue."

"Didn't you say she was inspired by your story? Maybe it's that simple." Mika smiled. "You are a great writer."

I smiled. "Thank you, but is there anything I'd write that would make you sink a hundred thousand dollars of newfound money into a building you hadn't cared about before?"

Mika shook her head. "No. There isn't. If I cared about something, I would have been fighting for it all along." She stared out the window, and I could tell she was thinking about how hard she fought to keep her store going now. Every month, it was barely enough, but that "barely" kept her going. "If I came into the money, I'd definitely build on what I had, but I don't think the money alone, even with a great article," she winked at me, "would be enough to get me to do something I hadn't been inclined to do all along."

"I think that's it. If I came into a lot of money, I'd invest it in my business, buy Sawyer a climbing gym for the yard, treat Lucille and Dad for all the help they've given us. I wouldn't start something I had never wanted to start before." It felt too convenient, this remodeling, but it wasn't really any of my business. "Still, I'll buy milk there and pick up a candy bar for a late-night snack when they open."

Mika raised her coffee, and I clinked my mug against it. "Here's to late night candy bars and convenient milk," she said.

"And maybe a side of pot to go with it," I joked . . . but even as I said it, something about my joke rang a bell. An alarm bell.

9

As soon as I got home, I called Santiago. It was late since I had needed a bit of time with *The Great British Bake-Off*, some strong tea, and a couch before I could drive safely home from Mika's, but I hoped the sheriff wouldn't mind since I thought it was his car that followed me into my driveway when I came home.

I'd considered walking over and tapping on his window, but that felt a little too much like the booty calls I'd seen in B-movies. I decided a call was better, especially if the person who opened the window was one of Santiago's deputies instead of him.

He answered on the first ring. "Glad you're home safe and sound," he said, and I could hear the smile in his voice. "Sawyer not with you tonight?"

"At his dad's." I tried to sound nonchalant. "Listen, I have a question for you, about Bailey Thomas's death. Do you have a minute?"

"I have a lot of minutes . . . a whole night full of them, in fact. Would you rather chat on the phone, or is this the kind of conversation that's better in person?" His tone was light, but his question was serious.

I paused and thought carefully about my response. I didn't want to give him the wrong idea. I really wasn't ready for a relationship, but I hated the phone . . . and for a conversation like this, I really wanted to be able to see him, to read his body language. "If you're up for a cup of tea on the front porch, I'll meet you there."

"Deal," he said, and a few seconds later, I heard his car door close.

I grabbed a couple of fleece blankets and wondered, not for the first time, how one woman had managed to accumulate so very many blankets in her forty-six years on earth. I tossed them in the folding chairs on the porch and turned on the kettle for some vanilla chamomile. By the time I came out with two mugs, Santiago was in the far chair with a blanket wrapped around his legs. He looked adorable, a realization I shoved way back into the dusty corners of my mind.

I handed him his tea and sat down and copied his blanket wrap. Then, I shifted slightly so I was facing him and said, "Why do you think Bailey Thomas was killed?"

If Santiago was surprised by my question, he didn't act it. "Someone wanted to keep something she knew hidden."

I took a long, deep breath. His answer confirmed my theory. "So you don't think it was someone with a grudge against her?"

He shook his head. "I don't. It was too clean a crime for that. Too perfect." He took a sip of his tea. "Someone acting out of anger would have been more volatile. This was planned, precise."

I nodded. "So what do you think she knew?" I realized I was probing pretty far into an active investigation, which was something my dad would definitely not approve of and that might put Santiago in a tough position, but I felt so tied to that woman's death . . . and to the store and the Scruggs family.

Santiago turned his head and looked at me. "Normally, I don't talk about cases with anyone outside the department." His voice was soft, and his eyes clear in the gentle light of the porch fixture. "But you know everything I do, maybe more, about the history."

I tried to look interested but not desperate, not desperate about anything.

"I can't tell you about angles we're looking into. That would be a breach of ethics, but I can tell you my overall theory." He studied my face for a minute and then continued. "I think it has to do with the pot, but I think the pot has to do with something bigger."

I looked out over the field down to the stream below and thought about what he'd said for a few moments. "Like someone has something bigger to hide than just a stand of pot in the woods?"

He nodded and sipped his tea as the sky above us began to clear and show the stars. "What's your theory?"

"I don't really have one yet, but there are a lot of things spinning in my head. What you say, though, it feels right somehow. Just not sure how yet." I wriggled back into my chair more deeply and held my mug under my breath to warm my face.

After a few more minutes of silence, Santiago said, "This is nice."

I sighed. It was nice.

THE NEXT MORNING, I decided to attend Bethel Church, both for the research for my future newsletter article but also to see if I might run into Mary Johnson again. Plus, I figured my appearance would build my cover more deeply and hide my inquiry into her part of the Scruggs Store story.

I got there early because it was going to be odd enough for a white woman to go to a black church that I didn't want to saunter in late. Dr. Martin Luther King, Jr., had said that Sunday was the most segregated hour of the week back in the 1960s, and that was pretty much still true, at least here in the rural South. I was going to stand out, so I wanted to stand out with respect, not the opposite.

One thing I knew was true of every church I'd ever been a part of: people had pews, and those people usually had pews at the very front or the very back. I took a seat about two-thirds of the way back on the outside of the church so that I could move out of the way if I had claimed someone's informally, but very seriously, reserved seat.

The church was pretty empty, but I was regularly early for, well, everything, so I was kind of used to it. But after five minutes and then ten, I started to get antsy. I tried to pass the time by reading the bulletin I'd picked up from the podium at the back of the church when I came in. I scanned the choice of hymns and was excited to know them all, at least a little, and I spent some time reading each name in the prayer list carefully. Then, I read the announcements, and finally, I read the fine print. When I was done, I was still mostly alone.

A couple of older women came in, greeted me, and then took their seats in the second pew from the front, and I immediately recognized their role in the church. They were the matriarchs, and as such, they always came early. I hoped I hadn't messed up their status by being there before them. A woman came down the side aisles and lit the candles under the hurricane glasses, and the organist started to play.

Ah, the prelude, I thought. My mom had been a church organist, and I always loved sitting in the quiet before the service and listening to her play. I sat back in the pew and took a deep breath . . . just in time to realize she was doing scales. She was just warming up.

That's when I finally read the *front* of the bulletin and saw

I'd come a full half-hour early for the service. No wonder I had been alone.

Still the pews began to fill soon after, and the organist launched into a zestful rendition of "How Great Thou Art." He was really, really good, and I could feel the punch of his feet against the pedals as he hit the final chorus. I could have listened to him play all day.

Soon, the pews were full, and I saw several people I knew from high school and around town, including Mary Johnson, who saw me, did a quick double take, and then waved before coming to sit in the only seat nearby, the pew right behind me. She leaned forward and asked, "More research?"

I nodded. "Figured the only way I could write about the parsonage was to know the church," I said quietly over my shoulder.

She patted me between the shoulder blades and then sat back. Soon, I was lost in the vibrant music, the enthusiastic response of the people in the pews, and the fiery but tender lesson of the pastor. The sermon was on second Corinthians, chapter one, which I remembered a few verses of, but hadn't thought much about. He preached on how in communities people lean on one another, giving compassion and comfort to each "as they had need."

He must have said "as they had need" twenty times, and each time, it burrowed a little deeper into me, like a harpist plucking a note to a song I didn't yet recognize. I listened carefully and was heartened in a way I hadn't been in a long while. I wanted to be one of those people who gave others what they needed, just as so many had done for me.

After the service, I tried to beat a quick retreat out the back, but Mary Johnson had me by the arm before I could get fully out of my pew. "Paisley, it's really good to see you here. You're really dedicated to your research."

If you only knew, I thought but smiled. "Well, it's not hard to research in a place like this. What a wonderful congregation." She looked around the sanctuary and said, "It really is. I wasn't always an easy person to love, but even when I was at my ugliest, the people here loved me hard, especially when I didn't want them to. These people, they pretty much saved me." I could hear the emotion in her voice.

I watched the small clusters of people hugging and exchanging dishes, some full and some returning empty. I saw children darting around and under the pews with parents and grandparents, both biological and adopted, keeping an eye out for everyone. It felt like family, and I wondered if they'd mind very much if one white lady joined them every week. "It's like a big family."

Mary laughed. "Yep, fights and all. You do not want to see us all at the Thanksgiving potluck, especially on election year." She shook her head. "But if you'd like to get a sample, a few folks are coming over to my house for lunch. I've made a big pot roast, and there's plenty."

Normally on Sundays, I tried to take some quiet time to myself, watch a movie, sew, tidy up the house, but as I looked around the sanctuary again, I thought that maybe what I needed was a little time with people. Plus, I still hoped to get a bit more information from Mary about Luther's family and maybe even the cash in the cabinet. "Um, sure, if you're positive you have enough? I could run up to the grocery store and get some bread or something."

Mary looped her arm through mine and turned me toward a tall, thin woman with ebony skin and said, "That woman right there, she makes the best bread in the state, and she's coming over with two loaves. We really have plenty. You can help me get things ready though if you don't mind?"

I appreciated the chance to contribute and squeezed Mary's arm against my side as I said, "I'd love that. Lead the way."

The two of us walked arm in arm out of the church, and while I saw a few smiles and knew that far more people were taking note than showing it, I felt completely comfortable. Well, except for the needling question I had about why Berlinda had disliked her sister-in-law so very much.

It had been obvious in the church that folks were not exactly bolting toward their cars, and so Mary and I took our time meandering up the block toward her house. "I loved what the pastor had to say about community supporting one another," I said.

"It's the thing that keeps me coming back," she said.

"The sermons?" I asked.

"No, the compassion. Like I said, those folks saved me." She pulled my arm a little tighter. "I was a very angry woman. Very angry when Luther died. Before Luther died." She slowed down her pace a bit as if she wanted to leave time to say all she needed to say.

"I didn't have the easiest childhood, and while I loved Luther, I resented how much time he had to put into that store to make it work. I also pretty much hated Berlinda for not doing what I thought she should do to help." She let out a long sigh. "I said and did a lot of things that alienated me from Luther's family. I still haven't spoken to Berlinda or George since Luther died."

I frowned sympathetically. "That must be kind of hard, to not have his family when you still miss him."

She smiled at me and nodded. "I expect Berlinda and George told you about me, and I expect they told you the truth. I was awful. So angry."

I didn't want to deepen any rifts in the family, so I just listened and made sounds to show I heard her. It's amazing what an *hmm* can do.

"I wish I could take back the things I did and said, but I have forgiven myself for who I was back then. I quite literally couldn't help myself. I was just so very angry." She grew quiet and thoughtful. "I've made peace with myself about it, but I haven't made peace with Berlinda. I need to do that."

I sighed. There was something about people reaching over to attempt to heal wounds that got me choked up every time I heard about it. I was soft-hearted, a trait I liked in myself, but I was also well-versed in history and in the ways that even personal resentments and pain could balloon into major tragedies for the people involved and the communities around them. "I expect, even if she doesn't show it right away, she would like that." That was all I felt comfortable saying, and it felt like enough.

"Paisley, I'll make this clear to Berlinda, too, but it feels important that you know it, too. I did love Luther, and while there were things about our life together, things I don't like to talk about, that were very, very hard, I did try to do right by him and his family . . . but I had to think of my son. Always him first."

I cleared my throat to keep from crying because I knew exactly what she meant. The choices I made, every single one of them, I did with Sawyer in mind. Other people couldn't always see that, but it was the truth. "That's why you never turned him in for growing marijuana?" I said very quietly.

She turned to me and studied my face before saying, "Yes. He wasn't using, and he wasn't selling himself. I didn't even let him use any of the money on our boy. And I knew if I brought it up, if I asked him to stop . . ."

"It would get ugly. Dangerous maybe." I knew the scenario well, too well.

She sighed. "Yes. He believed that money was our future, and I thought it was going to be our end." She swallowed hard. "I was going to leave at the end of the summer, find a place nearby for our son and me. Find a way for him to see his father but not have to live with him and the danger he brought into our home." She was staring off the porch of her house and into the past now.

"But then Luther was murdered, and you just left."

"I just left. I was devastated and even more terrified, and all I knew to do was get away." She looked up at the porch roof and took a deep breath. "I couldn't get far, just as far as this house as a matter of fact. It was cheap and sturdy enough, and my son and I made a home here."

"And you found your family here." I looked up the road to the church.

"We did." She smiled at me but then looked sad. "It was a terrible thing that happened to Luther. Absolutely terrible. But for me, it was a way out, and I took it."

"It meant freedom for you and your son." I took both her hands in mine. "I get it. Believe me. I get it."

"I suspect you do," she said. We stood quietly for a few minutes, hands clasped as we stared out at the mountains beyond town.

"You don't use your son's name?" I finally said.

A sad, sad smile passed over her face as she looked down at her hands. "I don't. It hurts too much. He died of cancer when he was fourteen."

I pulled her into my chest out of reflex. The very idea that Sawyer could die, let alone die that young stole my breath. "I'm so sorry. So, so sorry."

She squeezed me back and said, "His name was Henry. We called him Hank. Luther chose his name, and I always loved it."

I held her close a few minutes more as I thought about how a man had named his son after his own grandfather. Legacies live on, even when they are unsaid.

Dinner at Mary's house was lovely. Four other people from her congregation joined us, including the Bread Woman, whose name was Esther but who I thought I might call "The Bread Woman" forever because her bread was that good. We ate until we were ready to pop, and then they dealt out gin rummy. I was shy about my skills at first, but soon, all the games with my mom came back and I was dominating the table with whispers and woops of admiration from my fellow players.

About three o'clock, I finally excused myself, telling them I'd see them next week at church and asking if they'd be willing to share some stories about their congregation for my next article. All of them agreed, as long as it didn't disrupt the schooling they were going to give me in Rook the next week. It was a delightful afternoon, and I went back to the farmhouse feeling joyful in a way I hadn't in a long time.

A BLUE SEDAN followed me back home from the church, and when I saw the deputy in the front seat, I gave a small wave before I went inside. I felt kind of guilty to have all this protection when nothing was happening. I had begun to wonder if anyone had seen me at the Scruggs Store after all.

I thought about suggesting the sheriff call off the protective detail, but I figured he knew better than I did what was needed . . . and I was kind of hoping he'd be around more, even if it was just for work. Actually, I preferred if it was for work because that kept me from having to make up my mind about things, about him.

That afternoon, I had a million things that I needed to get done for work – website updates and auctions to check in on – but I'd learned in the time since my husband and I had split that what I needed most on the weekends that Saw was with his dad was downtime to just relax.

I made a plan – first a hot bath with a cozy mystery to read – I had the third book of Ellery Adams' Secret, Book, and Scone Society all queued up. Then a big bowl of popcorn, some cross-

stitch, and a binge-fest of *The Repair Shop* so I could admire all
the craftsmanship and bone up on some new-to-me history.

BY THE TIME Sawyer came back at eight the next morning, I was
well rested and ready to tackle toddler parenting again. My son
had had a good time with his dad, including a trip to Big Rocks,
his name for the local park that featured boulders he could
jump from. He was all words all morning as we played around
the farmhouse and seeded our garlic. I knew that fifty percent
of that garlic would not make it since Saw really liked to eat the
sprouts, but the joy of working in the soil with my son made
any loss of results well worth it.

After lunch, Sawyer, by some miracle of the parenting gods,
fell asleep in his bed instead of in the car, and so I decided to
take advantage of the time to do a little work. I started, as
always, with checking my email, and amongst all the random
list emails that I'd subscribed to over the years, I saw a few
notes that intrigued me, responses to my newsletter article. The
first one read, "Thanks for writing about this iconic Octonia
Store. I grew up going in there with my dad when he needed to
pick up a soda and sandwich for work on his roofing crew. I
miss that old place." It was signed Steve.

The next note reminisced about the store having Cheerwine when no one else did, and the author told me that they'd
bid on a case from my auction site just for the sake of good
memories and to support my work. I replied immediately with
a heartfelt thank you.

Most of the other notes were similar, bits of nostalgia and
support. But the last message I opened began with the line,
"Glad this place is gone. Too many lives were ruined because of
the horrors of that store and its owner. A den of iniquity. Good
riddance."

I read the message several times before I decided to forward it on to Santiago. It was probably nothing, but just in case, I wanted to send it on to the proper hands.

As I checked my online auctions and saw that I had, indeed, sold a case of Cheerwine to someone in the next town over, I mulled over the one note of hatred toward the Scruggs Store. I wondered if the person was talking about Luther Angelis when she mentioned the owner. That seemed the most likely option since most people who would have known the store when Alice Scruggs or Sheila Angelis owned it were long dead. The note needled at me as I worked.

Finally, I couldn't take it anymore and called the sheriff, hoping he checked his email as frequently as I checked mine. He answered on the first ring, "Hi Paisley. Got your note right here."

"Oh good. I'm sorry to bother you, but that note bothered me. It felt, well, kind of threatening somehow." I felt a little silly saying it, but it was the truth.

"No, you were right to send it over, and your sense of things is correct. Have you seen the paper today?'

I didn't get the local paper, mostly because it was barely ten pages long and predominantly ads. But I did try to scan the headlines on Facebook most days. "Not yet. Why?"

"Open the website," he said.

"Okay." I put in the URL and read the top headline. "Scruggs Store set to reopen early next year." I sighed hard. "Well, they didn't waste much time getting the word out."

"Nope, and someone who really doesn't want the store to reopen didn't waste much time making his feelings known. The store was vandalized this morning. And the vandal used the same phrase as in your note "A Den of Iniquity.""

I collapsed against my desk chair. "You can trace the email address, right?"

"Already in progress. We'll know who it was soon, so thank you."

I waited, hoping the sheriff would tell me more, maybe the identity of the vandal, but he stayed frustratingly quiet. After a few moments I said, "Well, then, I'm glad I could help."

"You did." He cleared his throat. "And when I have to testify about the case in court, I'll tell them you helped by sending the email, and I will be able to say, truthfully, that you didn't have any further part in that element of this investigation." I could hear the clear, direct tone in his voice.

"Got it," I said, feeling a little relieved that I wasn't just being shut out. This was about protecting the investigation. I knew Santiago had already toed the line, maybe even crossed it, with me, so I backed off.

"See you soon?" I said quickly.

"Tonight at six. My shift." I thought he was going to say goodbye and hang up, but instead he said, "Can't wait." Then the line went quiet.

I sighed. Sighed and smiled.

WHEN SAWYER WOKE UP, he and I spent the rest of the afternoon tossing sticks up into the cedar trees around the farmhouse. I did not understand the appeal of this game, but Saw loved it . . . and since it gave me something I could call exercise, I stuck with it for forty-five minutes. Then, when my son decided to wander off into the pastures around the house, I took up my watching post on the porch with a cup of quickly brewed peppermint tea. I let my mind traipse back over the questions I was still carrying: did my new friend Mary know about the money in her house or not?

I was leaning hard toward not knowing, but I found it very hard to believe that someone could stash away money in that space for so long without being caught. Just the logistics made it seem impossible. Surely, at least once, Mary would have walked in while Luther was putting the money in there, and if a huge cabinet sat in my living room, I would want to know what was in it. I realized I was more curious than many people, but still, I had to think she got inquisitive at some point.

I took a sip of my tea and resolved, once the case was closed, to just ask her. I wasn't about to disrupt Santiago's investigation with my own nosiness, but I knew the question would bug me if I didn't eventually get an answer.

That tiny bit of resolution set, I moved onto my bigger, more scary question – Victor Davison. He didn't look to be much older than forty-five, maybe fifty if he had really young-looking genetic material, so he could have been involved somehow with the whole pot situation.

I checked myself, though, because Santiago hadn't said anything definitive about Davison being involved. The sheriff certainly seemed to think that was the case, and the way Davison had approached me at Mika's shop didn't exactly set me at ease. But we hadn't made that link yet, and even casually, I was loath to assign guilt to someone without proof.

While I'd been lost in thought, Sawyer had located a mudhole, and while I didn't look forward to having to strip him on the porch before hustling him to the bathtub forthwith, I decided the damage was done and kept on with my musings.

I decided to consider other reasons that Davison had been at the store that day and why he had come to visit me at the yarn shop. Maybe he knew about the money and thought I had found it. Maybe he came to threaten me.

My cup of tea finished and me no closer to answers but much closer to being covered in mud, I zipped inside to grab one of the many throw-away towels I kept on hand for just such a moment and shouted, "Saw, come get dry, and I'll make spaghetti."

His head jerked up from whatever he was studying in the muddy water at his feet and gave me a grin that warmed my heart right to its center. Then, he did one last full-body jump into the puddle, fell on his rear end, and came charging at me with laughter preceding him. I took a quick look at what I was wearing and decided it would wash and grabbed my son as he launched himself up the porch steps. A huge hug and a mouthful of mud later, I had him stripped and into the bathroom where a warm tub with lots of bubbles was waiting. Being a mom to this guy was the hardest thing I'd ever done, but it was also, hands down, the best thing, too.

WITH SAWYER CLEAN, warm, and fed, he and I settled in for a few episodes of *PJ Masks* before bed. My phone chimed about six, but I wanted to enjoy this cuddly boy without distraction. It was only after Sawyer was asleep about eight that I responded to the sheriff's note.

"Porch available?" he wrote.

"Sure. Give me five." I slipped into my warmest pajama bottoms and a Messiah College sweatshirt that I bought on my first college visit almost thirty years ago. Then, I grabbed the lap blankets, the tray with the hot cocoa and marshmallows, and headed out.

The sheriff was already there, and on the small table between my porch chairs, he had placed a small Christmas cactus. I could see the tiniest hint of purple buds beginning, and I caressed her leaves as I sat down. "For me?"

"I thought you might need a little color once these autumn leaves fade." He looked at me from the corner of his eye. "I hope it's not too forward?"

"It's never too forward to give me plants. Thank you. She's going to bloom early, I think." I pointed the buds out to him.

"May her blooming be early and long," he said, and I felt like a blessing had been handed down to me.

We sat quietly for a few minutes, and I found myself doing the habitual listening that accompanied being a mom. But through the cracked front door, I didn't hear a sound from Sawyer. Unlike when he was an infant, once he was asleep now, he usually stayed that way for a few hours and sometimes, even, all night.

"I went to church at Bethel Baptist yesterday," I said and surprised myself. I hadn't been planning on divulging that particular bit of information, but now that it was out, I decided I might as well keep going. "It's a beautiful congregation."

Santiago nodded. "It is. Did you know that every Christmas they adopt five families in need and provide everything – from food to clothes to toys – for them? It's not something they advertise, but they've been doing it for decades."

"No, I had no idea." I felt teary just thinking about that. "How do they pick the families?"

"The pastor and I usually have a conversation."

I waited for him to elaborate, but he didn't. I asked. "You recommend the families?"

He shrugged. "I tell him about things I've witnessed – parents who have been incarcerated, families struggling with one member's addiction, chronic illness, widows and widowers – people I run into in the course of my work who just need a boost."

I sat back and looked at him as he looked out over the pasture, where just a few lightning bugs were still flashing their romance dance. "Is that hard?"

He turned to me. "Is what hard?"

"Seeing so many people who are hurting but being unable to help them yourself?" It had never occurred to me before that moment that police officers must have that experience often, and the tenderhearted ones must find that very difficult.

Santiago sipped his cocoa and said very quietly, "Yes."

I watched him for a moment and then let out a long sigh. I didn't want to overstep either, and the easiest way for me to do that was to ask too many questions. I'd done it before and found that, unlike me, most people don't want to go deep quickly.

But a moment later, Santiago said, "No one has ever figured that out before. Thank you." He didn't look at me, but his voice was soft, tender even.

I smiled into my mug. I hadn't scared him away. I took a moment to ponder what it meant that I'd been scared I would. When I felt myself fantasizing about nightly porch sits with this man I barely knew, I pulled up short in my train of thought and blurted, "Do you really think Davison was growing that pot?"

Santiago sat forward and turned his chair to face me. "I did, but now I'm not sure."

That set me back a minute. I really wanted to ask why, but I also didn't want to compromise the investigation.

"He came by the station today to apologize for scaring you." The sheriff looked at me intently. "Someone doing something nefarious, like growing illegal drugs, doesn't usually come into the police station of his own volition, let alone to apologize."

"So you're rethinking his connection to the store?" I asked with hesitation.

"I am." He set his mug on the table between us. "I asked him why he was at the store that day and why he came to see you at Mika's shop on Saturday."

"And?" I was balancing on the edge of my seat now, and the bar of the metal chair was digging into my rear in an uncomfortable way.

"He said that was between you and him."

I sat back hard and almost tipped the chair over. "Oh." I stared at the blue and green mug my dad had picked up for me at a local pottery fair last year and ran my fingers over the blue drips of glaze. "Do you think I should talk to him?"

A smile slid across Santiago's face. "If you want to know what he's up to as badly as I think you do, then, yes, I think you should talk to him."

I could feel the blush climbing up my cheeks, and I was glad I hadn't turned on the porch light.

"But," the sheriff added, "I want to be there. If it's okay with you, I'll call him tonight and suggest breakfast at eight? Can you find someone to watch Sawyer?"

"I can. While you make the call, I'll call Dad. He and Saw can go get pancakes."

Dad agreed readily to his Boy and Boppy Breakfast, as he called it. "Baba can go, too, if she wants?"

"No, she can't, honey," Dad said quickly. "This is our Boy and Boppy Breakfast."

"Yes, sir," I said and made arrangements to drop Sawyer off at seven-thirty.

When Santiago came back from around the side of the house where he had made his call, he said, "All set on my end."

"Good to go here," I nodded as I stood to gather the mugs and blankets. Then, I froze. "Wait, you'll have been awake all night. You need to go home and sleep in the morning."

Santiago waved a hand in the air between us. "I can sleep in the car." But then, as if he'd misspoken, he said, "I mean, I'm paying attention still, so it's not deep sleep, but it's enough."

I shook my head. "That settles it. You're on the couch tonight. That way, you're still doing your job, but you also get some rest." I looked at him to see his answer. "I don't mean to tell you what to do, but really, wouldn't this be better?"

He smiled at me. "I don't want to impose."

"You're guarding our lives, Santiago. It's not an imposition." I opened the door with my foot and said, "Come in. I'll get blankets and a pillow."

I watched him walk into the living room and go right to the wall of bookshelves that was filled with my favorite author's works, pieces of art made by friends, and some of my most precious cross-stitch pieces. He studied the book titles and then picked up a small framed piece that said, "Ebenezer."

I swallowed hard and went into the kitchen to gather myself. The piece was one I'd done for my mom years ago because it was her favorite name in the Bible. She said it spoke of what she called the nature of life – defeat, grief, and grace. On her refrigerator, she had written out, in her beautiful calligraphy, "Thus far hath the Lord brought me." One year, I stitched the word *Ebenezer* in a spiral of flowers and vines for her. When she died, I brought the piece home to remember her and how she taught me to look at life, as a path that is fraught but never solitary.

When I had pushed the tears back, I slipped past the sheriff, who was now studying my collection of thimbles, and grabbed a sheet, blankets, and a pillow from the trunk underneath the staircase in the hallway. I quickly made up the couch for him, after removing Beauregard and promising the cat space in my bed. Then, before I could say more than I wanted about my mom or about him, I said good night and rushed upstairs.

For a few moments, I stood at Saw's door and listened to the soft hush of his breath before I climbed into bed to read and to cry myself to sleep.

10

I wasn't asleep long, though, when I heard something. At first, I thought it was simply Sawyer coming down the hall to get into bed with me, like he did many nights. But then I realized that the rustling sound was coming from outside, right below my window. I stood up and looked out in time to see someone fling something at my house.

The sound of shattering glass brought me fully awake, and I bolted into Sawyer's room with my phone in hand. I was just about to dial 911 when I heard Santiago say, "Stay up there, Paisley. I've called for back-up."

I didn't know it was possible to be both relieved and more terrified by the same phrase, but "called for back-up" brought both of those emotions to the fore.

Fortunately, Sawyer's bed was against the opposite wall of the house, so he hadn't heard anything . . . and despite my huffing and puffing as I barreled toward his bed, he was still sleeping away. I slid carefully into bed beside him, grateful I had bought him a double bed instead of a single.

I wrapped my body around his to wait. It wasn't long before

I heard Santiago say, in a very loud whisper, "It's me. I'm coming up."

When he got to Sawyer's door, I made a psst sound and climbed out of bed to meet the sheriff at the door. I was not leaving my son. If someone was coming into this house, they had to go through me to get to my boy.

"I went out and saw just the taillights of a car leaving." He looked more puzzled than worried when I caught his face in the light from the hallway window. "It looked like a Buick or something."

"What does it matter what make of car it was? What did they do?" I could feel the tremors coming on as the adrenaline rushed through my system again.

He put his arm around my shoulders. "Let's sit at the bottom of the stairs. No one can get to Sawyer, but you need to sit down and get warm."

At first, I didn't want to budge, but as my shaking got worse, I realized he was right and let him lead me down the steps. Once I was sitting squarely on the third step, ready to take someone out at the ankle if they tried to get by, Santiago stepped into the living room and pulled one of the blankets off the sofa and wrapped it around my shoulders.

Then, he stood, facing the front door and the living room, where anyone would come if they came in through either of the house's other two doors, and said, "They were serious, Paisley. They threw bottles of gasoline all over the outside of your house. If I hadn't been here and scared them off, they would have burned the place down."

A surge of fear rushed through me, and I started to lose my breath. My gulps of air weren't helping as I imagined Sawyer and me caught upstairs in a blazing fire. Quickly Santiago scooted me over and sat down on the step beside me. "Put your head between your knees, Paisley . . . think about your feet on the floor. Feel the blanket on your shoulders. Focus on my hand on the back of your neck."

That third one did it. I could feel the warmth of his fingers as they massaged my neck, and the motion as well as the focus calmed my panic.

Once my breathing slowed, Santiago said, "The fire department is coming at first light to assess the situation and hose the house down." As he spoke, he kept pressure on my neck so my head stayed down as he rubbed the tight muscles in my shoulders. "I'd like to call your dad and ask him to come over. That way, he'll be here when Sawyer wakes up, and they can stay to watch the firetrucks before going to breakfast. Is that okay with you?"

Just the thought of my dad coming soothed me further, and I nodded under the sheriff's hand. "Yes, please. Call him."

"Okay, can I borrow your phone for his number?"

I still had my phone in a death grip, so I pried my fingers loose and handed it to him. "Don't scare him."

"Nope, I won't." He stood and then knelt down in front of me. "Sawyer is fine. You protected him. You are fine. Just stay here. I'll be right back."

I nodded and then as soon as he walked away, I crept back up the stairs to sit in Sawyer's doorway until dawn.

I woke with a start when I heard engines outside the house, and I was on my feet beside Saw's bed before I even knew I was moving.

Moments later, Santiago stood in the doorway with his hand held out, palm up. "It's light out, now, Paisley. The danger is past. Let him sleep. Let's get you some coffee."

I glanced down at my son and marveled, not for the first time, that someone who had needed to wake up every two hours to eat just months before was cruising into his tenth hour of uninterrupted sleep. I resisted the urge to kiss him so that I didn't risk waking him and followed the sheriff downstairs.

When I walked into my kitchen, I inhaled the beautiful scent of bread toasting, coffee brewing, and bacon sizzling. "I'm glad you made yourself at home," I said with a playfulness I didn't really feel completely.

"I hope that's okay. I figured you could use a good meal, and if your dad is like every other man I know from Octonia, he'll be wanting breakfast as soon as he wakes up."

It took me a minute to register what he'd said. "Dad is here?"

"In your bed. He came over right away, but you had already nodded off on the floor." Santiago set a hot mug of coffee with my cream and sugar set filled for the first time since we moved in right in front of me. "I offered him the couch, but he said since he'd been cleaning up after you for decades, he figured he could use your bed since you weren't."

I sipped my coffee and chuckled. "Can't argue with that," I said as I lifted the mug in a toast to him. "Thank you for this. For everything."

After pouring himself some coffee in my favorite "The Patriarchy Isn't Going to Fight Itself" mug, he sat down and added an almost invisible amount of milk to his coffee. "Just doing my job," he said.

"I hardly think cooking for your charges is part of your job," I said as I took another deep inhale of the bacon.

He blushed just the slightest bit as he took another sip. "You heard the firetrucks?"

Clearly, he wanted to change the subject, and that was just fine with me. "I did. Scared me awake."

"They aren't exactly quiet," he said with a smile. "I spoke with the chief. They recommend hosing the house thoroughly. Since your paint job is pretty new, they're confident most of the gasoline will wash away."

I nodded and then looked over at him in horror. "The gasoline will kill my grass, maybe the trees." I felt tears spring to my eyes as I thought how contaminated the ground would be after this.

Santiago reached over and put his hand on mine. "You don't need to worry about that. They are tarping the ground carefully, and they brought a clean-up truck to hose up the water. They'll take care of your place, Paisley." He squeezed my fingers and then put both hands on the mug.

Tears started to slide down my face as gratitude and exhaustion washed over me. But when I looked at the man next to me, I saw determination beneath his own fatigue, and I felt myself steady. "You've been up all night?"

"Some of it. I did catch a few more hours on your very comfortable sofa, though. Thank you for that." He smiled and stood to check our food.

When he opened the oven door, I saw a cookie sheet layered with cheese toast and let out a little yip of joy. I loved all cheese in any way, but cheese toast is one of those comfort foods that took me back to childhood breakfasts in the early mornings before school. Thank goodness, Santiago wouldn't force me to drink a full glass of milk, though. Mom had always insisted, and I had never taken to milk as more than a coffee enhancer.

"You like cheesy bread, I take it?" the sheriff said as he stood up and turned the bacon in the skillet.

"Cheesy bread? Is that your name for cheese toast?" I teased. "Are you four?"

"Forty-eight, but the name stuck from when I was four," he said with a small smile. "My nana always made this for us when we had a big test or had woken up from a rough night. Thought it might be good for all of us today, and you happened to have all the ingredients."

"Cheese and bread are staples around here," I said casually.

"I suspect butter and sugar are, too," he replied.

I closed one eye with suspicion. "Are you sure you aren't four, or maybe two? Sawyer would kill to have cheese toast with sugar."

"He won't have to kill anyone. It'll be ready for him when he wakes up." He refilled my coffee cup and then set another pot to brew.

At that moment, my dad came in looking a little ragged but also like embodied comfort. I had to resist jumping up and having him hug me tight. I knew he wouldn't mind, but I wasn't ready for Santiago to see just how much I needed my daddy.

When Dad put his hand on my shoulder and said, "Hard night, Baby Girl?" I squeezed his fingers and bit my lip to keep from crying again.

"The hardest. Sheriff Shifflett told you what happened?" I asked.

Dad took the mug of coffee that Santiago handed him and said, "He did." He shook his head and clenched his jaw, which was just about as close to swearing and calling people names as my father came. He was angry, but he wasn't about to let loose. It just wasn't his way.

"I have our entire team working on this, Mr. Sutton. We'll get him." Santiago didn't look up from where he was moving the bacon onto a paper towel on one of my plates.

"I have no doubt," Dad said, "but if you need someone to take care of things off the record . . ."

"I appreciate the sentiment," Santiago said as he handed Dad a plate of steaming bacon and cheese toast, "but you know I cannot officially condone such an offer." He winked at me and turned back to get my plate.

The three of us gathered around the peninsula and ate in silence as the sun crested the mountain and shone down through the living room windows. Outside, I could hear the fire crew working, but I was too nervous to look . . . and even more nervous that they weren't starting to spray things down yet.

Finally, I couldn't contain my anxiety and went to look out the kitchen window. The firefighters were all standing around their trucks sipping steaming mugs of something that I assumed was coffee. "They're just standing there, Santiago," I nearly shouted.

He came over and put his arm lightly across my shoulders. "I told them to wait a bit so that Sawyer could sleep. They're keeping an eye on things, though, Paisley. Nothing is in danger." He spoke so softly and certainly that I instantly felt better.

As if on cue, tiny feet pattered down the stairs and into the kitchen. "Mama?" Saw said as he rubbed sleep from his eyes.

"Hey Buddy," Dad said from where he sat on the kitchen stool.

"Boppy here?" Sawyer asked as I picked him up.

"He is," I whispered into his warm head. "He's got a treat for you."

"Two treats actually," Dad responded as he came over. "Two surprises. Want to go have breakfast with Boppy?"

Sawyer, still struggling up out of sleep, said, "Where Boppy?"

"How does Michael's sound?" Michael's was a classic diner that both Dad and Sawyer loved.

"Let's go," Sawyer said as he tried to wriggle out of my arms.

"Wait, Lovebug. We have another surprise," I said.

"Another 'prise. What is it?" He stared at me with giant, brown eyes.

I pulled the blinds open and pointed. "Look."

"A firetruck." He leaned forward and pressed his nose to the window. "Two firetrucks. Five firetrucks."

"Two firetrucks. They're going to wash our house." I was

very glad that Sawyer wasn't old enough to know that it wasn't typical for the firetruck to wash down a house.

"Go?" Saw said to urge the fire trucks to action.

"We're ready then," Santiago nodded and stepped onto the porch. He raised one finger and swung it in a circle over his head.

The firefighter closest to us nodded and gave the same signal to the two teams behind him, and within moments, they had two hoses stretched across the yard and were blasting my house with hundreds of gallons of water.

"Guess we'll find out if the roof holds," Dad said with a smirk.

"Don't even joke," I said sharply.

"We in a waterfall," Sawyer said with a wide grin on his face.

I took a deep breath and let myself see it like he did . . . and suddenly, the moment was magical. The sun streaming through the droplets of water, the sound of rushing water surrounding us, the presence of three people who cared only that we were okay. "It's magic, Sweet Pea," I whispered.

"It's magic," he said back.

Within minutes, the entire house was hosed down, and the flood recovery truck had sucked up most of the water they had expended. As they drove away, I stepped out into the yard with Sawyer, and we looked back at our house. It looked just the same as it had the night before, but now, it was glistening in the early morning sun.

"Magic, Mama," Sawyer said.

I smiled again. "It is, Little Man. Now, it's time for you to have some magical chocolate chip pancakes with Boppy." I carried him over to Dad's car and strapped him in. "Boppy's in charge, okay?'

"No, I in charge," my young son said with a glint of mischief in his eye.

I gave him my best "Mom Look" and then said to Dad, "Good luck . . . and thanks."

Dad gave me a quick hug and then climbed into the car saying, "How about whipped cream on your pancakes?"

I could hear Sawyer's cheers of joy as they rode off up the driveway.

When I turned back to the house, I saw Santiago with a rake smoothing the gravel that had been churned up by the firetrucks. "You don't have to do that?"

"My pleasure. Feels good to move around a little." He finished the last tire track and turned to me. "But I'm afraid I do have to ask a favor."

"Anything," I said without thinking. But much to my pleasure, the only reaction I saw from Santiago was a slight reddening of his ears.

"Do you mind if I use your shower? I smell a little bit like bacon and gasoline." He smiled.

"Truckstop cologne is the hot new trend," I said. "You sure you want to wash that off?"

"I saw some baby shampoo in your bathroom. Maybe it's the fountain of youth?"

"If you're aiming for younger, you might want to try the bubble gum-scented bubble bath while you're in there." I headed for the house. "I'll get you some towels."

Santiago followed behind me. "Why do people always say that? How many towels are necessary for most people to shower? I only use one."

"It's a towel set thing, I guess. If I'm giving you a bath towel, I'm including the hand towel and wash cloth, too." I bounced my head back and forth a bit. "Maybe that's it . . . but I do hear some people use one for their heads and one for their bodies."

"Hedonistic luxuriants, those people," Santiago said as I handed him a matching bath towel, hand towel, and wash cloth. "Bubble gum scent here I come."

I watched him walk around the corner to the bathroom, and then I sunk to the couch and lost myself in a mixture of tears and laughter for a few minutes.

AFTER I HAD FINISHED my own shower, during which Santiago cleaned up from breakfast, he handed me another mug of coffee, this time laced with cinnamon, and said, "Are you up for meeting Davison? If not, I can easily reschedule for later today or tomorrow."

I looked at my phone which I had decided to plug in and charge up just in case I needed it for yet another emergency. It was just seven-thirty, and I felt like I had been up for hours . . . because I had. "Actually, it would be good to have a distraction."

"Okay, if you're sure. One of my deputies is here to keep an eye on the house. I don't think the arsonist will come back, but we want to be sure." He ran the dishcloth over the counters one last time before walking to the door. "I'll drive if that's okay with you. You could use a break, I think."

I stared at him as he walked out, too stunned to walk. I hadn't even thought about the fact that we might still be in danger.

Then, I ran after him and said, "Actually, do you mind if I drive? I could use the feeling of control, I think."

He stopped, looked at me, and said, "Sure. Let me just let Deputy Wilson know?"

I smiled and then, at the spur of the moment, decided to go back for Beauregard. He would have been content to sleep off the bacon-grease coma that he was nursing, but if it was possible that horrible person was going to come back, I didn't want him in harm's way.

When I walked back out to the Subaru with Beau on his leash, Santiago doubled over with laughter and then said, "It's you. You're the woman with the cat on the leash."

"I am," I said as Beau jumped, with a lot of side eye for the sheriff, into the backseat. "You've heard of me?" I flipped my ponytail and then snagged the blanket off the front seat so that the sheriff's khakis didn't get covered in gray cat hair.

"Actually, yes." The sheriff studied my face as he sat down. "You don't know?"

I started the car and said, "Don't know what?"

"You're famous in town. They call you the Cat Walking Lady."

I stopped at the end of the driveway. "Who calls me that?"

"Everyone, Paisley. Everyone," Santiago said with a chuckle.

I wasn't sure whether to be offended or flattered, and I decided I didn't have the energy for offense. "I'll have T-shirts made, then."

"I'll wear that shirt with pride," the sheriff said as we drove up toward town.

DAVISON WAS WAITING for us when we arrived, and I noticed that he was nervous. He shifted from foot to foot and didn't quite meet my eyes. "Thanks for coming," he said quietly as I sat down across from him with a large vanilla latte. I was soon going to be able to supply the town's electricity needs from my own caffeinated electrical field, but I needed to stay alert for this conversation.

"Sure. You wanted to see me?" I said, trying to sound casual and feeling anything but.

"Um, yeah, I wondered if you had found it." He still wouldn't meet my eyes, and he was rocking back and forth in his seat.

Suddenly, I saw something that fear had blinded me to earlier. Victor Davison was probably on the autism spectrum. What I had interpreted as threat before was actually just part of his disorder, which made it very hard for him to read other people's emotions and physical actions. Instantly, I felt more at ease. "Found what, Victor?" I said.

My neighbor growing up had autism, and people were often afraid of her because she sometimes had really big emotional outbursts over things many people would not think that important. But I had learned that when she had big feelings it was because things felt big to her. I thought it was possible that being friends with Audrey had taught me empathy and compassion better than anything else in my life. I still talked to her regularly, even though she now lived in Utah with her partner and their son. When I needed to be reminded that how I felt mattered, she was the person I called because she never failed to remind me that everything about me mattered.

Davison looked up at me for a second and said, "The money. Luther hid a lot of money in his house."

I glanced at Santiago, but I couldn't read his expression. He did nod, though, and I took that as a sign that he wanted me to continue.

"We did find it, Victor. It's safe. It'll go to the rightful owners, Luther's sister." I wanted to touch Victor's hand, but I held back.

"It's going to Berlinda?" he said. "That's who should get it."

I nodded. "Yes, Berlinda will get it." I took a deep breath and hoped it was okay with Santiago if I asked this question. "How did you know about the money, Victor?"

"Luther told me about it, told me to be sure Berlinda got it if something ever happened to him." Victor was sitting still now, and he looked calmer now that he knew he'd fulfilled his duties.

"You knew Luther?" I said with a smile.

"Oh yeah," he said. "I did all the maintenance at the shop. Worked for Luther for years . . . until . . ."

"Until he died," I said. I looked over at Santiago, and he was smiling at me. He made a small gesture with his hand to tell me to keep going. "Well, then, I bet Berlinda would like to know that. Did you hear that she and George were going to open the store again?"

Victor jolted. "Yes, I did. I need to go now." He stood up and turned to go. Then, he turned back, "Thank you," he said before he strode out the door.

I sat back and took a long sip from my latte before I spoke. "You knew he was on the spectrum?" I asked Santiago.

He nodded. "After he came by yesterday, I suspected, but I talked with his dad, and he confirmed."

"You wanted me to see for myself so that I wouldn't be afraid of him?" When he nodded, I said, "You realize that could have really backfired, right? I mean a lot of people are afraid of people with disabilities. That was a risk."

"Not with you, it wasn't," he said.

I gave him a wan smile. "I appreciate the vote of confidence in my self-awareness, but you didn't know that. I could have been a real horror in that moment." I understood what the sheriff had expected to see and was glad I had delivered, but I'd seen too many people underestimate the tenacity of prejudice to discount the possibility of that in myself.

"Well, maybe I should have told you." He looked at me, and when I raised an eyebrow, he said, "Okay, I should have told you. Forgive me?"

I nodded. "But let's talk about what he was concerned about. Luther told him about the money? Does that strike you as odd?"

He shrugged. "Maybe. But tell me why it seems odd to you?"

I took a minute to figure that out for myself and said, "I guess because if Luther was doing something so secret, why would he tell anyone at all?"

"That's a good point," Santiago said as he stood to take our mugs to the counter. "But maybe Victor was the only one he could trust . . ." His voice faded away as he looked out the window.

"What?!" I stood up to follow his line of sight.

The sheriff shook his head slightly and then turned to me. "Oh, nothing. Just thought I saw something, but I must have been mistaken."

We walked to the door of the coffee house, and I was about to ask him if he wanted me to take him back to his car at my house when he said, "Can your dad keep Sawyer a bit longer?

"I expect so, why?"

"Are you willing to go back to the Scruggs Store with me to look at something?"

I furrowed my brow and studied him for a second before I said, "Don't you have deputies for this kind of thing?" I didn't mind going. In fact, I was excited to go, but my dad's caution and Santiago's statement about court felt too important to just ignore.

"I do, but one of them is guarding your house, and the other is doing everything else. Besides, you have a good sense about you," he looked at me and must have still seen my skepticism because he added, "and you have already been in the house and so you aren't seeing anything new or disturbing a crime scene since we removed the tape two days ago."

"Alright, alright," I said with a laugh. "Let me check with Dad."

My father is not always the most "on-top" of the cellphone situation, but to his credit, when he was with Sawyer, he responded quickly. Today was no different, and when I texted, *Can you keep Saw busy for another couple of hours?* His reply was immediate.

Already on our way to the goat house. The "goat house" was my son's name for a local Mennonite market and petting zoo that also, gladly, allowed children to play on the swing sets they had available for sale. Combine that with the fact that the donut truck was there on Tuesdays, and Sawyer was going to be busy until lunch.

If he falls asleep on the way back, you'll drive him? I replied.

Yep, picking up Lucille to help keep me awake. See you about two, Dad texted in what was a tome of texting in his world.

"I'm all yours," I said and then immediately blushed.

"Well, that just makes my day," Santiago said with a small smile as he climbed into my passenger seat.

I started the car and pulled out toward the store, curious about what we were looking to see there but also content to just enjoy the ride without having to answer the question "Why?" every time I slowed down, hit a puddle, or stopped speaking for more than three seconds. "Why you got quiet, Mama?" was a Sawyer classic.

But I did get one question on the ride, and it made me crack up. "I hope this doesn't offend you, Paisley, and tell me if it does. But would you mind if I we stopped at the car wash so I could vacuum your car? I feel really bad that I'm pressing goldfish into the seat and floor mat."

I looked back at Beauregard who knew very few words in human but *did* know vacuum, a word of terror, and said, "Buddy, I'll hold you, and we'll be quick." Then I looked at the human next to me, "I love that idea. I have dreams, sometimes, of having my car clean. Those dreams are usually short-lived, however."

Santiago laughed. "I have no delusions that this will last, but at least it'll be tidy for a few hours."

"Indeed, and sometimes a few hours of tidy are all this toddler-mama needs to rebalance the universe a little."

Beau was remarkably easygoing at the car wash, even as I used the fancy coupon my dad had given me over the summer to get "the works" in the automatic car wash. Sawyer would love the lights, and I decided to build ten dollars a month into my budget just for the car wash and the vacuums as a treat to myself and my son.

The vacuuming took almost no time, and Beau didn't even want to get out but moved willingly around the car as the vacuum chased him. Five hundred goldfish and six sticky fruit snacks later, and we were on the road again. The cleanliness of my car, brought about by my efficient use of some baby wipes to clean the dash and display coupled with the vacuum, made me giddy.

But when we pulled up to the Scruggs Store, my elation vanished because the vandalism was worse than I imagined. The words were scrawled in bright orange spray paint all across the front of the building. Someone had wanted to send a clear message.

Santiago got a call just as I parked, so I got out and took a closer look at the damage. It was pretty intense, especially if Berlinda wanted to keep the original wood on the front of the building. I didn't think the paint would come out of the old wood because the material was so dry that the paint had been absorbed deeply. I didn't know much about refinishing wood, but these boards looked too thin to be planed down . . . and besides, the cost of that would be, in all likelihood, prohibitive.

I tried to catch Santiago's eye as he continued his conversation from the passenger seat of my car, but he was very intent on what the caller was saying. So I decided to take a look around the outside of the building on my own. I figured there was no harm in that, and since I hadn't really walked around the exterior, I was curious.

I headed left around the building, toward the door that went straight into the Angelis house and saw that the door was still barred with police tape. I moved on past the side porch to the rear of the building. I could clearly see the small window to the foyer, the big window over the kitchen sink, and then the two smaller windows that let the back bedroom look out over the hillside.

The other side of the house had two additional windows, one more in the back bedroom and one in the master bedroom, where I'd found Thomas's body. The siding was in pretty good shape back here, so I wondered if maybe Berlinda could borrow some of this wood to replace the vandalized pieces up front . . . or maybe she'd just paint the whole building again. I was so eager to see what she was going to do.

I knew that Santiago would call out when he was ready for me, and I didn't intend to wander far. But the view from the back of the house was pretty breathtaking, so I walked a few feet toward the ravine behind the building to get a view down into the woods.

The forest looked old, not virgin timber certainly, but old enough to have shaded out most of the understory. A few mountain laurels shone waxy in the dappled sunlight, but mostly, the space under the trees was open except for fallen leaves and dead-fall trees. It was beautiful, quiet.

When I walked a bit further into the woods and headed north, the brilliance of the green leaves was hard to miss. In fact, the marijuana stand was so bright I was shocked no one had seen it from the road before. But then, given that a murder had happened in the store, that the building had sat empty, and that I'd passed by here hundreds of time and never seen this stand myself, maybe it wasn't so unusual.

I was curious, though, never having viewed marijuana up close and personal, so I listened one more time to see if Santiago was calling for me and, hearing nothing, headed over. It was pretty impressive and way taller than I'd imagined. It felt a bit like walking into those bamboo stands they have around some of the exhibits at the National Zoo, well, like walking into that bamboo if I was at an outdoor Dave Matthews concert. I could definitely get a contact high if I stayed too long.

I started to make my way back out when I heard a rustling behind me, and it wasn't the bouncing footfall of a squirrel or the scramble of a possum or skunk. This movement was something big, and in these parts, big things in the woods were either people or bears. I wasn't interested in seeing either, so I turned tail and moved as fast as I could without making a huge racket myself.

When I cleared the stand of pot, I began to run in earnest because whatever, whoever was behind me was clearly headed my way, and I did not want to be caught by person or bear. Not in this situation. Not in most any situation actually.

The leaves were slick, though, and my slightly-too-big shoes that I'd bought on sale from a Facebook ad were not the best for escaping danger. I kept gaining ground on the steep slope and then sliding back a few feet. At this rate, I was going to have to try to take my pursuer out at the ankles if I had any hope of escape.

Finally, I was about to crest the hill when something grabbed my left ankle, a very human-handed something. I kicked out with my right foot, hoping to dislodge the grip, but doing so only threw me off balance, and I face-planted in the leaves. I thrashed and flailed with all my might, and I was just taking a deep breath to scream when a massive hand clamped down over my mouth.

The person holding me turned me over, and when I looked up, I saw George Jefferson. It took me a minute to register that it was him, but when I did, a wash of relief passed through my arms and legs, and I went limp.

I should have realized that "Don't scream" isn't normally what someone says when they're in a friendly sort of way, but I was just so pleased to recognize him that it didn't register that his words were a threat, not a comfort, at least not until he flipped me back over with my face in the leaves so he could grab my arms and bind them behind me. Then, reality started to sink in.

I thought about screaming, I really did, but George was a big man, a huge man, and I didn't stand much of a chance against him if he decided to fling me back down into the ravine, where I would almost certainly hurt myself badly and maybe break my neck. My son needed me to be able to take care of him, so I resolved to survive ... and right then, surviving meant staying quiet.

George pulled me the few remaining feet to the house and then shoved me to a sitting position below the kitchen window. My brain was spinning as I tried to think of a way to let Santiago know what was going on, but my phone was pinned to the ground in the back pocket of my jeans. Survival now depended on me protecting myself, and I was finally getting good at that after years of putting myself last.

"George, what is going on? Are you okay?" I decided to try to act like I was worried in the hopes that George would think me naïve. I had found that men are often quite willing to believe this about women. Normally, I'm infuriated by that fact, but today, I decided to use it.

George had been peering around the side of the house toward the entrance, but now he spun back around. "Am I okay? What do you mean? Of course I'm not okay. You're about to ruin everything."

I took a deep breath. "How, George? What have I done?" I kept my tone curious, even, like I did when Sawyer was pushing my last nerve with a tantrum over something like the number of chocolate chips in his cookie.

"You were just supposed to go into the store to salvage, not the house. We didn't tell you that you could go in the house." His voice was agitated, raspy.

I let out a long slow whistle. "I had no idea. I'm so sorry. I thought I had permission to go into the whole building. I'm so sorry I violated your trust." I felt like I sounded honest, but I couldn't be sure because my brain was all over the place. George had not wanted me to go into the house because he had killed Bailey Thomas and left her there.

"Well, you didn't," George said as he took a seat on a fallen log at the edge of the woods. "If you hadn't gone back there, all of this would have been over. But now, now, there's going to be a new store, and my operation is going to be compromised. After all these years . . . after all I've done."

I glanced over toward the marijuana stand and felt all the pieces of this terrible history slide into place. "You killed Luther." It wasn't a question, just a statement, and one I wished I'd had the forethought not to say out loud.

"See, I knew you'd figured it out. I thought I was going to have to make another visit to your house—"

"YOU! You tried to burn my house down with my son and me in it?! YOU did that!" My rage was white hot, and I was on my feet before I even realized it. "You!!" I charged at him with all the anger and fear in my body, and by luck, I caught him off guard. When my knee connected with his groin, George Jefferson fell over like one of those toy punching bags for kids.

It only took me a second to realize now was my chance, and I bolted around the building and right into Santiago, who was just coming from the front.

"Back there. It was George Jefferson. Go!"

Santiago didn't hesitate. He drew his gun and moved. I managed to grab my phone from my back pocket and then drop it on the hood of my car by spinning around. I shouted, "Siri, call 911." Siri, like the sheriff, didn't hesitate, and I – grateful that Siri and 911 work even where cell service is nonexistent – heard the dispatcher at the police station answer.

Just then, a shot rang out from behind the store, and I heard the voice on the phone say, "Was that a gun shot?"

For a split second, I thought about running back to check

on Santiago, but then I thought of Sawyer. "Yes, shots fired at the Scruggs Store. This is Paisley Sutton. I'm with Sheriff Shifflett. Send help."

"On our way, Paisley. Sit tight." The call stayed live, and I managed to wiggle open my car door and get inside before locking the doors. I felt cowardly, but my first priority was to be Sawyer's mother. I tried to comfort myself with the fact that I hadn't seen a gun on George, but it was only when I saw the sheriff leading a limping and handcuffed George Jefferson around the front of the store that I actually took a full breath.

I scrambled out of the car as the sheriff moved Jefferson closer and said, "Do you mind?" He gestured with his head toward the back seat.

For a second I hesitated. I didn't like the idea of blood on Sawyer's car seat, but then, I got a little perspective and said, "Sure."

Santiago shoved the huge man into the space between the passenger's side rear door and the car seat and slammed the door shut. "You've got the child locks on, right?"

I smiled. "That I do."

"You're a good mom, so I figured." The sheriff stepped toward me. "Now, are you okay?"

"Terrified and eager to see my son, but yes, I'm okay." I slumped against the hood of the car after Santiago freed my hands. "I called for help."

"Good," the sheriff said and then leaned beside me. "Later, you'll tell me what you were doing back there?"

"Sure. Later. Porch. nine p.m.?"

"Sounds good." He said as we slumped against each other and caught our breaths.

WITHIN MINUTES A PATROL car and an ambulance arrived. The EMTs patched up the wound in George's arm and then insisted on taking a look at me. I was fine, if still shaky, so they transported George to the hospital with the deputy who had been guarding my house along for the ride.

After Santiago drove me to the station to get my official statement, he took me home, ostensibly to pick up his own car but also, I could tell, to be sure I was safe and sound and resting. After getting me set up on the couch with episodes of *The Good Place* as well as a cup of tea and my cross-stitch, he left in my car again, this time to get it detailed at the expense of the department. "If you thought the vacuuming took care of that toddler grime, wait until you see it after this," he said wryly before heading out with a deputy in his car and the other following behind the entourage of vehicles from my quiet farmhouse.

As soon as I heard the cars leave the driveway, I let myself have a good long cry and decided to follow the sheriff's advice and just rest. I picked up my stitching and settled into the couch for some laughter . . . and then I woke up when Dad brought Sawyer home.

My boy must have been prepped that I'd had a hard day because he came in quietly and just snuggled up against me. "I love you, Mama," he whispered as he rested his head against my shoulder.

I swallowed my tears and said, "I love you, too, Sawyer. Did you have fun with Boppy?"

Then, my son launched into one of his fabulous tales of jumping off roofs and landing in puddles so big he "went under," and soon, I was laughing and asking for more . . . and all felt a little bit more right in the world.

Dad looked exhausted, so he went up to my room to get a couple hours of sleep. And I roused myself for toddler time, even though what I really, really needed was a good friend and the couch for the rest of the day. "This is parenting," I thought and clambered down to the floor to play blocks.

A few minutes later, though, a knock sounded on my door, and Lucille came in with a cake carrier, what looked like a lifetime supply of playdough, and a smile. "Baba's here, and I'm ready to play."

For the forty millionth time that day, tears came to my eyes, and I beamed at her. "Oh yay! Baba is here," I said to Sawyer as he toppled yet another tower of blocks.

"Baba, play blocks with me," he commanded.

"Of course, I'll play blocks with you," my stepmother said before she turned to me and whispered, "Chocolate cake with white icing" and nodded toward the kitchen. After helping myself to a slice, I slid back onto the couch to watch the tower-building extravaganza and sew after figuring out exactly how many episodes of *The Good Place* had streamed along without me while I slept. I'd want to catch up later.

While Lucille helped Sawyer make the most epic tower ever, I finally let myself think about George and just how scary my morning had been. But the fear wasn't what sat with me now. It was worry, about Berlinda. I couldn't believe she had known about any of this, and I wished I had a way to comfort her when she found out.

I texted Santiago one word: *Berlinda?*

Just talked to her. She's okay. But she could use a friend.

I sighed. I really wasn't up to going out, but I would find the strength. *I'll be there in twenty.*

No, you won't, his reply said, and then my phone rang.

"Paisley Sutton, you are not coming down here to support the wife of the man who tried to kill you. That is ridiculous." Santiago's tone was firm.

I wanted to protest, to say I would come, but I just couldn't. I was too exhausted, and I just wanted to be with Sawyer. "Okay," I said. "But surely there's someone who could come be with her." Then, I felt a glimmer of an idea, a possibly misguided one, but somehow, I thought this might work. "I'll call you right back."

I dialed and within minutes, Mary Johnson was on her way to the station to support her former sister-in-law. She hadn't even hesitated when I'd explained, in brief, the situation. All she'd said was, "I knew this would blow up eventually. I'm on my way."

When I told Santiago, he said, "I'll put them into my office. Give them some time. Thank you. See you later."

11

The rest of the day went by quickly as Lucille made dinner and Dad took Sawyer outside to climb something. I grabbed a glass of white wine and let myself be taken care of for a little while. About six, just as dinner was finishing, there was a knock on the kitchen door followed by Mika's smiling face. "I brought more wine," she said before immediately coming over and hugging me. "You okay?" she asked as she studied my face.

I nodded, too afraid I'd cry again if I spoke. "Lucille is making chicken parmigiana, so of course I'm okay."

"Thanks for inviting me, Lucille." She held up the bottle of wine. "Pour you some and give you a refill."

I shook my head. "I need to stay clear-headed after you all leave."

"Leave?" Mika said. "I'm not leaving until the morning. I'm on auntie duty overnight, my friend."

I felt a tiny shred of weight slide off my shoulders. "Well, then, by all means, pour away."

Dinner was amazing, especially because Sawyer *loved* the chicken parm almost as much as he loved the "sketti." And he was thrilled to have four of his favorite people together in the same room.

After dinner, we all played with Sawyer's giant alphabet train as we tried, in vain, to teach a two-year-old his letters. Then, Lucille cleaned the kitchen, and she and Dad headed out for the night. "We'll come tomorrow," she whispered as she hugged me goodbye. "Give you some more time in the morning."

I squeezed her tight in gratitude and then turned back to my son. "Ready for your bath?"

"Auntie Mika, take a bath with me," he ordered.

I looked at my friend and sighed. "Sawyer, Auntie Mika didn't bring her bathing suit, Love Bug."

"Are you kidding? Of course, I did. I was given a heads up, and I am ready for a bath." She scooped up the squealing toddler and headed toward the bathroom. "Saw, there's not room for three of us in your bathroom, so let's let Mommy make popcorn, okay?"

"Okay. Popcorn please," he said as he hung upside down in my friend's arms.

I did as requested, and after he and Mika dried off and wiped down the walls of the residue from their massive splash battle, we all settled onto the couch to watch *Masha and the Bear* before I took Sawyer up for bed. Mika offered, but there were some things Sawyer wasn't ready to give up with me yet, and bedtime was one of those things.

He was wiped out from his exciting day with his people and fell asleep in minutes. As I walked down the stairs, I said a quiet prayer of thanks for all the folks who had gotten me through. Then, I collapsed on the couch with Mika and cried.

That was short-lived, though, because we had a new season of *Kim's Convenience* to see . . . and we were thick in the third episode when I heard a knock at the door and froze.

"What?" Mika said. "You weren't expecting someone."

From behind the couch, she had grabbed a baseball bat that, apparently, she'd stored there while I got Sawyer into bed. "Call 911."

I pushed the bat down into her lap and said, "Actually, it is the police." I glanced at my phone. Sure enough, nine p.m. "It's Santiago. I forgot he was coming by."

Mika grinned. "Okay, well, I'll go get into bed with my book so as not to disturb you."

I blushed. "You can actually stay here. We're going out on the porch." I cleared my throat. "It's kind of our thing."

"Oh, you have a thing, then." She wiggled her eyebrows as she grabbed the remote from my hand. "Well, then, I'll be watching *Buffy*." My best friend loved *Buffy, The Vampire Slayer* above all else, and so I left her to her show and opened the kitchen door.

Santiago stood there with two huge mugs and a single tulip. "I thought maybe you would prefer not to have to even turn on the kettle."

"And the flower?" I asked, feeling a little cheeky.

"Just some joy at the end of a hard day." He handed me the flower and went right into the living room, where he grabbed the blankets off the arm chair, gave Mika a smile, and headed straight to the porch.

I dropped the bright red tulip in a glass of water and followed him, ignoring Mika's giggles as I went by.

The tea he brought was flowery but light, and since he'd remembered I liked lots of cream and sugar, it was somehow perfect. I sipped it as the sky darkened and the bats began to circle in the farmyard. "Seems like this day has been eight days long," I said.

"Well, today did start yesterday," he said with a small laugh.

"Oh my word. You've been awake since yesterday. I can't believe you're here."

"Nowhere else I'd rather be," he said with a quick glance at me. "But I won't be staying long. I just wanted to check on you and give you an update, if you want one."

I sat forward. "I do. How did things go with Mary and Berlinda?" I had been thinking about the two women on and off all day.

"Well, I think Mary was taking Berlinda back to her house for the night, and then I'll see them tomorrow to figure out what they want to do about the building now, all things considered." He stared out across the pasture.

"Oh yeah, maybe Berlinda doesn't want to fix it up now. I could totally understand that."

"She wants to fix it up, with Mary as her partner. That much I do know. It's just that they're thinking the plans might be bigger, more like a small restaurant and convenience store sort of thing." He smiled. "I told them I'd help them figure out zoning and permits and such."

I chuckled. "That's nice of you. Please let them know I'll help as much as I can, too."

"Will do." He settled more deeply into his chair and said, "Okay, I'm ready."

"Ready for what?" I looked at him and tilted my head in question.

He smiled. "For all your questions. Hit me."

"You won't answer anything I shouldn't know?" I really, really didn't want to make his job harder or hurt the case.

"I will not."

"Okay, did Mary know about the money?"

"Yes. Not the extent of how much, but she knew it was there. She also knew it was drug money and didn't want to have any part of it." He said matter-of-factly.

I sat for a minute and let that sink in. I'm not sure I would have been able to have her fortitude, especially as a single mom, and then a single mom with a very sick child, but I respected her choice. "Okay, good. But Berlinda did not?" I held my breath as I waited for the answer.

"Right. She had no idea. But Mary thought she knew all this time."

"Ah, and that's why Mary was so cold to Berlinda."

"Right again. Mary didn't know that George was running things, just that Luther was dealing out of the store. Since he and Berlinda were so close, she figured that Berlinda must have known, too."

I sat back. "But it was all the men's doing. I see." I paused for a minute. "But that money was older than that. It wasn't all drug money."

"No, it wasn't. Mary told me that Luther's mom and grand-mother had been putting away every spare penny for years so that they could expand the store." He cleared his throat. "She said that's why he got into the drug business with George because he wanted to speed things along."

I groaned. "Good intentions. Bad plan." I rubbed my eyes as the fatigue of the day and the sadness of the story settled deeper into me. "And George? He was in charge of things."

Santiago put his hands on his knees. "That's where it gets more interesting. Apparently, he's been running operations like this out of small stores all along the Blue Ridge for years now. Once we had the MO figured out, I called a few other police departments and asked them about remote convenience stores and marijuana. Sure enough, four of them had suspicions that people were dealing out of the stores. George had a drug ring going strong."

"But why keep the stand here in Octonia if the store was gone?"

The sheriff looked over at me and smiled. "You ask good questions. I wondered the same thing and was curious about where they were processing the pot for sale. Drying it. Packing it, etc."

"And?"

"Turns out our quiet road is quite the drug highway. His crew would come by to tend the stand and harvest from it as needed, and then they'd head down to Nelson County to process and distribute. The stand was just too valuable to let die out."

I nodded. "Okay, one last question. Luther wanted out? And George killed him?"

Santiago ran his fingers over his hair. "Yep, Luther knew Mary was going to leave him if he didn't go straight, so he told George he was done and that he'd have to take out the plants behind the store. Clearly, George did not like that idea."

I groaned. "So much death and heartache over some plants."

"Over so much cash," the sheriff corrected.

"Oh, right. Man, this means that the cash can't go to Berlinda, doesn't it?" I sighed. "Because it's drug money, I mean."

"Well, I put in a call to the attorney general. I think he's willing to work out something if she and Mary testify against George."

"And she will?"

Santiago stood up and helped me to my feet. "We'll see. I think so."

I walked Santiago down the porch steps and around the house toward his car. "Thank you for coming over and for answering all my questions," I said quietly. "Oh wait, one more. Why didn't your office take the plants out when you first found them?"

"Another good question, Ms. Sutton. We actually were hoping they'd be able to be used for medicinal purposes and were just waiting for the okay to release them to a distributor in DC. Now, though, they'll be harvested as evidence."

"Sort of doubly green recycling?" I said with a smile.

"Something like that."

"Well, thanks again, Santiago, for everything." I met his gaze and felt my heart kick up a bit, even through my fatigue.

"My pleasure. Always, Paisley." He took my hand and kissed it softly. "I hope we get to have lots more of these talks . . . but maybe not about murder and such."

"I'd like that," I said as he climbed into his car. "But slowly okay?"

"Any way you'd like," he smiled and waved as he drove away.

I watched him leave and then braced myself for Mika's questions when I came in. She had fallen asleep on the couch, however, so I covered her up and made my way to bed. Sawyer was going to be up early when he remembered Mika was here.

OVER THE NEXT FEW DAYS, George was indicted for two murders, Bailey Thomas's and Luther Angelis's, and everyone fully expected him to be convicted when his trial came up in a few months. Berlinda was heartbroken, of course, but Mary's companionship helped, especially since Mary had managed to survive heartbreak herself when her son Hank died.

Over the next few months, the Attorney General did release the funds from the Jefferson case, and Berlinda and Mary opened Ma-Ber's, a charming gas station with a country flare, great hot plate food, and all the conveniences us rural folks appreciate having at our fingertips. Both women moved into the house behind the store, which they fixed up with a great kitchen and two comfortable bedrooms.

For my part, I helped find vintage décor for the store walls and was on hand to help paint and polish as I was able. Sawyer even helped out a little by filling the drink coolers on the night before they opened, a job he took very seriously because

Berlinda had promised him a whole bottle of chocolate milk that he could drink "by self" when he finished.

It felt good to see the store open and the community come out to support these two women who were following in the footsteps of the women before them. They hung the photo of Alice and Sheila at the front door to remind them of their roots.

On the first morning the store was to open, a caravan of vehicles filled the parking lot before the announced opening time. Berlinda, Mary, Mika, and I watched with delight as people lined up to come in. At the front of the line, next to the sheriff, was a white woman with silver hair and a lean frame. I recognized her from around town, but I couldn't remember her name. She was beaming, though, so when Berlinda unlocked the door and said, "Come in," the woman walked right up and said, "Berlinda, we're cousins. I couldn't wait to be here to support you."

Berlinda stared at the woman and then glanced over at me before turning back to the woman and saying, "You're Sheriff Lewis's granddaughter. Let me get you some coffee, Cousin. I'm so glad you're here."

I swallowed the lump in my throat and scooped up Sawyer. "We helped do a good thing here, Love Bug," I whispered in his ear.

He squeezed me tight and said, "Wow. Look at all these people who want chocolate milk."

"Exactly, Saw. Look at all these people," I said with a laugh.

Read the next book in Paisley's adventures, *Bobbins And Bodies* - https://books2read.com/bobbinsandbodies.

GREAT READS AND A FREE NOVELLA

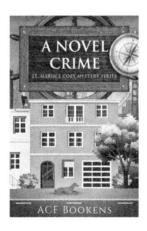

Join my Cozy Up email group for weekly book recs & a FREE copy of *A Novel Crime*, the prequel to my St. Marin's Cozy Mystery Series.

Sign up here - https://bookens.andilit.com/CozyUp

ALSO BY ACF BOOKENS

St. Marin's Cozy Mystery Series

Publishable By Death

Entitled To Kill

Bound To Execute

Plotted For Murder

Tome To Tomb

Scripted To Slay

Proof Of Death

Epilogue of An Epitaph

Hardcover Homicide

Picture Book Peril

Stitches In Crime Series

Crossed By Death

Bobbins and Bodies

Hanged By A Thread

Counted Corpse

Stitch X For Murder

Sewn At The Crime

Blood And Backstitches

Fatal Floss

Strangled Skein

Aida Time - Coming in January 2023

~

Poe Baxter Books Series

Fatalities And Folios

Massacre And Margins

Butchery And Bindings

Monograph and Murder - Coming in March 2023

Spines and Slaughter - Coming in April 2023

ABOUT THE AUTHOR

ACF Bookens lives in Virginia's Southwestern Mountains with her young son, an old hound, and a bully mix who has already eaten two couches. When she's not writing, she cross-stitches, watches YA fantasy shows, and grows massive quantities of cucumbers. Find her at acfbookens.com.

f facebook.com/bookenscozymysteries

Printed in Great Britain
by Amazon

23186472R00116